D0371853

Never Grow Up

A **BAXTER FAMILY CHILDREN** *Story*

Never
Grow Up

WITHDRAWN

KAREN
KINGSBURY
and TYLER RUSSELL

A Paula Wiseman Book

Simon & Schuster Books for Young Readers

NEW YORK • LONDON • TORONTO • SYDNEY • NEW DELHI

SIMON & SCHUSTER BOOKS FOR YOUNG READERS
An imprint of Simon & Schuster Children's Publishing Division
1230 Avenue of the Americas, New York, New York 10020

Karen Kingsbury is represented by Alive Literary Agency, 7680 Goddard Street, Suite 200, Colorado Springs, CO 80920 www.aliveliterary.com

SIMON & SCHUSTER BOOKS FOR YOUNG READERS
is a trademark of Simon & Schuster, Inc.
For information about special discounts for bulk purchases, please contact Simon & Schuster Special Sales at 1-866-506-1949 or business@simonandschuster.com.
The Simon & Schuster Speakers Bureau can bring authors to your live event. For more information or to book an event, contact the Simon & Schuster Speakers Bureau at 1-866-248-3049 or visit our website at www.simonspeakers.com.
Book design by Laurent Linn
The text for this book was set in ArrusBT Std.
The illustrations for this book were rendered digitally.
Manufactured in the United States of America
0121 FFG
First Edition
2 4 6 8 10 9 7 5 3 1
Library of Congress Cataloging-in-Publication Data
Names: Kingsbury, Karen, author. | Russell, Tyler, author.
Title: Never grow up / Karen Kingsbury and Tyler Russell.
Description: First edition. | New York : Simon & Schuster Books for Young Readers, [2021] | Series: The Baxter family children ; [3] | "A Paula Wiseman Book." | Audience: Ages 8-12. | Audience: Grades 4-6. | Summary: While Kari Baxter eagerly awaits a meteor shower and frets over what she wants to be when she grows up, Ashley gets an idea for how to keep her siblings from growing up too fast.
Identifiers: LCCN 2020029435 (print) | LCCN 2020029436 (eBook) | ISBN 9781534412217 (hardcover) | ISBN 9781534412231 (eBook)
Subjects: CYAC: Family life—Fiction. | Brothers and sisters—Fiction. | Meteor showers—Fiction. | Christian life—Fiction.
Classification: LCC PZ7.K6117 Nev 2021 (print) | LCC PZ7.K6117 (eBook) | DDC [Fic]—dc23
LC record available at https://lccn.loc.gov/2020029435
LC ebook record available at https://lccn.loc.gov/2020029436

Dear Reader,

*Hello again! We are so happy that you loved our first two Baxter Family Children books—*Best Family Ever *and* Finding Home! *You made them both big hits, and you were sure to tell us just how much those books meant to you. Thank you for that! The letters, posts, colored pictures, and reviews were heartwarming to me and to Tyler. One of our favorite comments was from a third-grade boy who said, "I will watch every day to make sure you write what happens next."*

*And so we bring you this third book in the Baxter Family Children collection—*Never Grow Up. *Now that the Baxter Children are settled in their new lives in Bloomington, Indiana, this book will give you a glimpse of how important it is to appreciate your days as a child. The days of being young.*

Writing about the Baxter children and seeing them grow up in their loving and supportive family has been an incredible joy for us. I've been writing about the Baxters for many, many years—the years when Tyler was growing up! Now, though, these books take us back to a simpler time when the Baxters were children, when they were growing up and finding their way. Sort of like flipping through the pages of a family photo album.

Like with Best Family Ever *and* Finding Home, *this third installment in the Baxter Family Children's story will have you laughing and smiling and thinking about what matters most—faith, family, and figuring out life along the way.*

In fact, we like writing about the Baxter children so much, there just might be more books in this collection somewhere down the road!

Enjoy . . . and always keep reading!

*Love, Karen
and Tyler*

BROOKE BAXTER—an eighth grader at Bloomington Middle School in Indiana. She is studious and smart and happy about her family's move. Like before, she has her own room.

KARI BAXTER—a sixth grader at Bloomington Elementary School. She is pretty, kind, and ready to make new friends—even if that means starting a new sport. Out in their huge backyard, Kari and Ashley find the perfect meeting spot for the family.

ASHLEY BAXTER—a fifth grader at Bloomington Elementary. When life gets crazy, Ashley is right in the middle of the mess. Always. She is a dreamer and an artist, open to trying new things. She sees art in everything, and is easily the funniest Baxter child.

ERIN BAXTER—a third grader at Bloomington Elementary. She is quiet and soft-spoken, and she loves spending time with their mom. She has her own room in the new house.

LUKE BAXTER—a second grader at Bloomington Elementary. He's good at sports, but sometimes he's a little too risky. Most of all he's happy and hyper. He loves God and his family—especially his sister Ashley.

Never Grow Up

Meteor Madness

KARI

Kari Baxter's head was somewhere in the clouds.

Nothing very unusual about that. Kari was more of a dreamer than most kids in her sixth-grade class. Only this time being in the sky was the exact right place for Kari.

Her teacher, Ms. Nan, was talking to them about meteors. Not from a science fiction book. But actual balls of fire streaking through the real-life sky over their heads. Kari could hardly believe it.

Ms. Nan stood in front of the class. "Next month we'll have a meteor shower over Blooming-ton, Indiana." The teacher's eyes lit up. She was a big fan of meteors, apparently. She looked down the rows of students. "We'll do a countdown until then, and on that night each of you will spend an hour viewing the meteor shower from home."

Excitement welled up in Kari. An in-person meteor shower! Right here in Bloomington! She couldn't wait to tell her family. Her four siblings would also want to count down the days, Kari was sure.

She gazed out the window and imagined the night sky covered with streaking lights, and she couldn't stop smiling. Kari liked school. She was good at all her classes. But this wonderful news took learning to an entirely new level. Kari turned her eyes back to Ms. Nan and listened to every word.

"Boys and girls, I assure you this will be an unforgettable cosmic event." Ms. Nan sat on the edge of her desk. "Who has seen a meteor shower before and what do we know about them?"

Liza's hand shot up first. Liza was one of Kari's new friends, and her teammate on the school's swim team.

"You've seen a meteor shower, Liza?" Ms. Nan looked impressed. "Was that here in Indiana?"

"Well, not exactly." Liza enjoyed talking. "Last summer we went to Washington State for Fourth of July and my uncle set off a hundred fireworks." She made a grand gesture with both arms over her head. "All across the whole sky." Liza smiled and lowered her hands back to her sides. "And that, I believe, was very much like a meteor shower."

Ms. Nan blinked. Like she wasn't sure what to say. "I see." She nodded. "Very nice, Liza." She looked around. "Has anyone seen an actual meteor shower? With meteors?"

A kid named Jake raised his hand. He played drums in the school band. "Ms. Nan, aren't meteors falling stars?"

"Hmm." Their teacher tapped her knee. "Good thought, Jake. They are kind of like stars. Let me show you." She walked to the blackboard. "Okay." Ms. Nan drew a small circle. "Here we have Earth. That's us." She drew lots of smaller circles around Earth. "These represent other planets and stars. Even debris."

"Debris?" The question came from Mandy, who sat next to Kari. Mandy was another of Kari's friends, and also a fellow swimmer. Mandy never fell in the mud or got dirt on her dress at recess. She wrinkled her nose. "You mean . . . like trash?"

Ms. Nan turned to Mandy. "Well, kind of . . . There could be rocks, or comets and asteroids. This is typically what we call meteors." She drew some rocks with fire coming off of them. "A meteor shower is caused by streams of this natural cosmic debris entering Earth's atmosphere at extremely high speeds."

High speeds? A splash of fear hit Kari.

Up until that moment Kari had figured she would watch the meteor shower from the middle of their huge front yard. Or on the big rock by the stream behind their new house. The rock was flat and it was the best place for Kari and her older sister, Brooke, and her younger siblings—Ashley, Erin and Luke—to sit and talk.

But now she wasn't so sure. Maybe they'd be safer inside.

Kari raised her hand. "Ms. Nan . . . That sounds dangerous. What if meteors crash into Blooming-ton and we blow up?" Kari's heart beat harder. "Maybe we should take cover."

4

"Well . . ." Ms. Nan crossed her arms. "I suppose a meteor shower could be dangerous. But it isn't likely." She smiled. "I'd say we don't need to worry."

Kari tried to imagine how the event would look. "So as the rocks and garbage come into our . . . atmosphere . . . ?"

"Yes, atmosphere." Ms. Nan nodded. Patience was her strong suit. "*Atmosphere* will be one of our spelling words next week." She hesitated. "Anyway, yes, a meteor shower happens as rocks and *debris* enter our atmosphere."

"With flames around them?" Kari still wasn't convinced this was a good idea.

"Yes." Ms. Nan smiled. "Exactly."

"When is it?" Kari tapped her desk. "How many days?"

Ms. Nan laughed and walked over to her calendar. "Forty-one days. Just over a month."

Kari's shoulders sank a little. "So . . . Bloomington might be destroyed in forty-one days?"

"No." For a second, Ms. Nan laughed out loud . . . but then she seemed to get control of herself. "Kari. Bloomington will not be destroyed in this meteor shower. Scientists can predict that sort of thing."

Their teacher started talking about Mars and Jupiter, which gave Kari time to think. Ms. Nan wouldn't lie to them. Surely the meteor shower wouldn't destroy Bloomington. And that meant Kari could be excited again.

A real meteor shower right over their very own city!

"All right." Ms. Nan stood. "Let's do free reading now. Then after lunch we'll talk about our next assignment. It's called: *When I Grow Up.*"

Kari's mouth went dry. *When she grew up?* Why would Ms. Nan want them to think about that? Sixth grade was hard enough without thinking about growing up. She raised her hand superfast.

"Yes, Kari?" Ms. Nan looked confused.

Kari swallowed. "Do we have to decide today? What we'll do when we grow up?"

"No." Something about Ms. Nan's voice made Kari relax. "You don't have to decide. I'll explain everything after lunch."

"Yes, Ms. Nan." Kari remembered to smile. She didn't want to panic, but she was struggling to get her head around this assignment. Sometimes she wasn't sure what she wanted to do next week, or what she wanted to have for lunch. The idea of trying to decide what she wanted to do when she grew up was scary.

She didn't know how else to put it.

When their teacher was back at her desk, Kari grabbed her journal from her backpack. Journaling was her favorite. She flipped through the pages until she found the next blank one and then, with a quick breath, she began to write:

A meteor shower is coming to Bloomington! In just forty-one days! It sounds like the prettiest light show ever and I bet God has the best seat in the house that night. November 15. Yep. That's the day. Ms. Nan says not to worry that the flaming meteors will destroy our city. So that's good. Also, I have to think about growing up. It's our assignment this afternoon. But the truth is . . . I have no idea what I want to do. Dancing, maybe. Or soccer. Here's my secret: I'm not even sure I like being on the swim team, which I haven't told Liza and Mandy. What if they don't like me if I'd rather dance? I can't think about it. Actually, maybe I'll study meteors.

"All right." Ms. Nan stood. "Lunchtime." The bell rang and the students lined up at the door. Kari finished her journal entry.

Okay. I gotta go. Consider this the official meteor shower countdown.
41 DAYS UNTIL THE METEOR SHOWER!

2

The Falling Leaf

ASHLEY

On this superfantastic, most excellent day, Ashley was a leaf caught in the wind.

Spinning and dancing and twirling in circles, trying to make it all the way up to the clouds. Round and round, over and over again. She spun faster. The clouds were so close she could touch them.

Ashley's unlikely new best friend, Natalie, stood on the school playground, eyes wide, just watching her.

"Things are looking up for me, Natalie! I'm almost dancing on the clouds. I'm a leaf caught in the wind!"

"You're gonna get sick." Natalie sounded concerned. "We just ate."

Ashley kept spinning. "No need to worry, Natalie, my friend." Her words came out a bit wobbly. Her twirling took her feet in bigger and bigger circles.

"I *am* worried!" Natalie yelled this time. "What if you fall? Everyone will see you!"

The spinning was catching up to Ashley. "No falling for me." She kept doing circles, arms out to her sides. "Dancing to the clouds is the best leaf activity for this happy Tuesday. You don't know what you're missing, Natalie."

"Stop, Ashley!"

Suddenly dizziness came over Ashley like a heavy blanket. "That's . . . why I—" Ashley blinked a couple of times and came to a sudden stop. "Whoa. I need to sit." She bent over her knees but she couldn't stop herself. And in a sudden thump she collapsed to the ground.

Very much like a leaf, actually. A heavy leaf.

Natalie hurried over. "I told you!"

"I'm fine. Just a little woozy." Ashley exhaled. She caught a glance of the rest of the class near the kickball area. Apparently no one had noticed.

"Are you okay?" Natalie stooped down and stared. "Your cheeks are green."

Ashley pulled her knees to her chest and squeezed her eyes shut. "Whew!" The world was still spinning. "I should *not* have had that second slice of pizza."

"It was *my* slice." Natalie raised her eyebrows.

"But you don't like pizza." Ashley opened one eye and squinted at her friend. "So a second slice for me made perfect sense."

Natalie still looked worried. "Maybe not on a twirling day."

"True." The spinning playground was finally slowing down. Ashley leaned back, using her arms as support beams. She still felt sickish, but her pizza was staying in place. So that was good.

All of a sudden she started to giggle. Soft at first.

Natalie raised her eyebrows. "Ashley?"

"I'm fine." Ashley's giggle became a laugh. "These things always happen to me, Natalie. Have you noticed that? Which is kind of funny, right?"

"You're the only person I know who wants to be a dancing leaf."

"A leaf dancing to the clouds." Ashley tilted her head back and stared at the sky. "I was so close."

Natalie got down on the ground next to Ashley. She leaned her head back and looked up as well. The two of them sat there, watching leaves drift to the ground. "Ashley, you'll make it to the clouds next time." She smiled. "There's no better leaf than you."

"Thanks." Ashley stood, brushed her hands on her jeans, and helped Natalie to her feet. "That's why we're friends, Natalie. You see the real me."

"I'm glad you didn't break your leg." Natalie put her hands on her hips. "You need to be healthy for Field Day tomorrow."

"What?" Ashley almost dropped to the ground again. "Field Day? How could I forget?" She ran in place for a few seconds. "That's my very best day of the year!"

Natalie laughed again. "Better than Christmas? Or your birthday?"

"Okay, not the very best." Ashley ran in place again. "But it's up there."

A familiar voice called from behind her. "Are you okay?"

Ashley did a half spin and saw Landon Blake. He had a basketball on his hip. Landon had been a menace at the start of this year. But not anymore. He had become another unlikely friend.

But in that moment, Ashley realized there was a problem here.

If Landon had seen her fall, then the whole class probably had, too. Ashley used her most dignified voice. "I'm fine, thank you very much."

"It looked like you fell." Landon stared at the dirt on her knees. "See?"

Ashley felt her cheeks get warm. In a quick rush she cleaned the dirt from her knees. Natalie hadn't moved since Landon showed up. Like she was in shock.

Ashley tilted her head. "I was a twirling leaf. Dancing up to the clouds." She paused. "But like all leaves, I'm supposed to end up on the ground."

Natalie let out a little laugh.

"Okay." Landon grinned. "Sure. That makes sense."

"Right." Ashley nodded. "Good. I'm glad we figured that out."

"What are you doing for Field Day?" Landon dribbled his basketball a few times.

Was he trying to battle her? "A lot." She crossed her arms. "At my old school I was pretty much Queen of Field Day."

"Funny." Landon tossed the basketball to Ashley. His eyes were still smiling. "Because around here, I'm King of Field Day."

"Really?" Ashley caught the ball and took a step closer to Landon. "I guess we'll have to see about that." She tossed it back to him. "And yes, that's a challenge."

Landon dribbled the basketball between his legs. "Challenge accepted." His friend Chris was calling him from the court across the school yard. Landon waved. "See ya!" He dribbled the ball back to his friends.

Ashley turned to Natalie. "We have a lot of practicing to do." Ashley noticed her friend's long blue hair ribbon. Very softly, Ashley pulled one end of it. "We'll need this."

"No." Natalie stepped back. "It's mine!"

"I'll give it right back." Ashley grabbed at the ribbon again. "It's for Field Day."

Natalie thought for a few seconds. Then she sighed. "Fine." She took the ribbon from her hair and handed it to Ashley. "What does this have to do with Field Day?"

"It's for the three-legged race, of course! The day's most difficult event!" Ashley positioned herself shoulder to shoulder with Natalie. "You have to be totally *in sing* with your partner. Like when you sing a song together and the words happen at the *exact* same time."

"You mean . . . *in sync*." Natalie laughed again. "Working together is *in sync*. Not *in sing*."

"Hmm." Ashley hummed a few notes. Natalie might be right. "Either way, we have to move at the same time." She bent down and tied their side-by-side ankles together with Natalie's blue hair ribbon. "Perfect."

"I don't know . . ." Natalie looked worried again. "What if—"

The bell rang.

Ashley stretched her hands over her head, one way, then the other. "We have to hurry."

"We can't do this now!" Natalie seemed ready to untie the ribbon.

"To the classroom! Here we go!" Ashley stood tall, eyes straight ahead, like she was at the starting line of the Olympics. "One . . . two—"

"Wait!" Natalie shouted. "Who are we racing?"

"Us!" Ashley raised her hand in the air. "One, two, three . . . Go!" And like that they were off. Natalie kept up, which surprised Ashley. Together they did a sort of hobble skip to the classroom. Not the smoothest three-legged race. But neither of them fell. And as they tagged the wall at the same time, Ashley knew something. Not only was Natalie a new best friend.

But she was the perfect partner for Field Day.

Mr. Garrett was Ashley's teacher. They hadn't gotten off to the best start. Ashley accidentally spilled ice cream on Mr. Garrett's head at the back-to-school night, and there was the time she got lost at the school field trip to the zoo. Also her teacher hadn't given her the sea animal she wanted in the class ocean presentation. But at the end of the day, he was a fun teacher. And she was thankful for that.

Now Mr. Garrett stood at the front of the room holding a stack of books. "We have a new class book to read." He held up the cover. It had a lovely drawing of a pirate ship. "J. M. Barrie's classic, *Peter Pan*."

The class started talking at once. "I love *Peter Pan*." In the chair next to Ashley, Natalie clapped her hands. "This is our best book yet!"

Ashley searched her head. She had seen the *Peter Pan* movie, but it was a long time ago. Pilots and fairies and pixie dust. Something like that. Also a boy who wanted to become a crocodile. Ashley lowered her brow. No . . . that wasn't it. A boy who didn't want to throw up. Or was it—

"Peter Pan is the story of a boy who didn't want to grow up," Mr. Garrett explained as he passed out copies of the book.

"That's it!" Ashley slapped her desk. The other kids turned to look at her. "Not throw up. The boy who wouldn't *grow* up!"

The story was coming back to Ashley now.

"Peter had a bunch of pilot friends, right?"

"Pirates, Ashley." Mr. Garrett frowned. "Not pilots." He sighed. "And they certainly weren't his friends."

From the back row, Chris shouted, "Pirates are my favorite!"

No surprise, Ashley thought. Based on his aggressive and sometimes hard-to-handle attitude, Chris might be an actual pirate.

Elliot, another one of Ashley's new best friends, raised his hand. "Peter Pan can fly. Is that right?" Elliot talked with a bit of a lisp because of his braces.

Mr. Garrett looked impressed. "Good, Elliot. Yes."

"He goes high up into the clouds and then on into space. Like aliens." Elliot talked very fast and breathless. Especially when it came to space and aliens. Elliot loved aliens.

"No, Elliot. Not aliens." Mr. Garrett walked through the classroom giving out books to the students. "In the story, Peter goes on a fantastical adventure up to the clouds."

18

Natalie nudged Ashley. "Like you!" she whispered. "Spinning your way up to the clouds."

Ashley felt a thrill run through her. Natalie was right. She was just like Peter Pan!

Mr. Garrett was still passing out books. "Peter Pan takes with him a group of siblings, the Darling children."

Ashley raised her hand.

Mr. Garrett paused. "Yes, Ashley?"

She drummed her fingers on the top of her desk. "Why were they darling?"

Mr. Garrett tilted his head to one side. "Excuse me?"

"You said they were darling." Ashley threw her hands in the air. "So. What made them that way? Were they teeny tiny babies? Those are darling. Or were they loved by everyone in their village? Sometimes *that's* a clue that someone is darling."

"No, no." Mr. Garrett laughed and handed Ashley her copy of the book. "Darling is their last name. But good question, Ashley."

Ashley studied the picture. She loved the glittery stars and the kids flying through the sky. If the cover

was anything like the book, then she was in for a real treat. She looked at the cover again. *Peter Pan*.

Ashley thought about Peter Pan and his life. Never growing up. Flying in the clouds. Going on adventures with pirates. He didn't have to worry about new schools or making friends or gymnastics. Or falling on the playground.

It seemed like the perfect life.

In the van on the way home, Ashley pulled out her sketchbook and began to draw. She sketched a different picture every day. This time it was herself midspin. One hand held a sword, to fight off pirates, of course. And with the other she threw pixie dust in the air. Like Peter Pan. But this time Ashley wasn't on the ground like a regular girl.

She was dancing on the clouds.

3

Brooke's Breakdown

KARI

One day, Kari was going to write a book about her family. *The Baxters*, she would call it. And when she did, their new house was going to be a character. That's how much she loved it.

That afternoon when they got home from school, after her siblings had gone in, Kari stood outside the two front doors and stared at the house. The white porch that wrapped from the front to the back, and the windows to each of their bedrooms. Plus the pond and stream and the million miles of green grass and trees that surrounded the place.

She loved everything about it.

Kari ran inside and took her backpack upstairs. They had only moved here a few months ago, but already her bedroom was her favorite place in all the world. The room she shared with Ashley. She dropped her bag and stared out the giant window. Beneath it was a built-in reading bench. Where Kari had already spent a thousand hours.

Yes, the house would be a very special part of her book, for sure.

Dorothy in *The Wizard of Oz* had said it best: There really was no place like home.

Kari hurried back downstairs with her journal.

Mom was slicing apples for their snack. "Who has homework?" She pulled a plate from the cupboard. The house smelled like warm cinnamon.

"Not me." Luke's arm was still in a cast from falling out of the backyard tree. But he could use his fingers now. He unzipped his backpack, pulled out a wadded-up sheet of paper and handed it to Mom. "I finished it in the car. So can I go play outside?"

"Son . . ." Mom uncrumpled the paper. "You need to be more careful with your schoolwork."

Mom pressed the wrinkled page along the kitchen counter. It didn't help.

Luke grinned. He had lost a tooth last night, so he had a big hole in the front of his mouth. "At least I did it."

"No. Not at least . . ." Mom put her hands on her hips. "You are a Baxter. That means we do our best. No matter what." She looked down at Luke's shoe. "And please, tie your shoelace."

Luke covered up his laugh. "Yes, ma'am."

"Go play." She handed the messy page back to Luke. "But be more careful next time."

"I will!" Luke seemed to be a little more cautious as he put the page back into his backpack. Then he ran outside. Within seconds Kari could hear the sound of the basketball on the pavement.

Mom sighed. "Making baskets is more important to that boy than making good grades." She looked at Kari. "What can we do?"

Kari shrugged. "He does make most of his shots."

This time the laugh came from Mom. "True."

Brooke wasn't home yet, but none of the other kids had homework. Mom set a plate of apples on the kitchen table and joined Kari, Ashley and Erin there. She looked at the girls. "I need to make participation prizes for Field Day. You three want to help?"

"Yes!" they all said at once. Doing projects with their mother was always a fun way to spend the afternoon.

Mom explained the project. "Each student who participates will get a bag with a letter from the principal and a number of prizes." Mom organized piles of gel pens and small notebooks, colorful pencils and yellow smiley-face key chains. The last pile consisted of small candy bars, plus there was a stack of letters. "I'll put the candy and a letter to the parents inside a bag and pass it around the table. You girls fill it with one item from each pile."

It took them a few tries to get the rhythm of the assembly line down, but once they had it, they were able to work and talk at the same time.

"How were your days?" Like always, Mom sounded happy. "Give me the highlights."

"Good." Erin answered first. She was in charge of the colorful pencils. "I sat next to a new friend at lunch. His name is Max." Erin passed the bag to Ashley.

"Max. That's nice." Mom placed a parent letter and a candy bar in a few of the open bags to get the assembly line started.

"I had a dancing day." Ashley was getting behind on the key chains. She picked up her pace. "What does the winner of Field Day get?" She looked at their mom. This seemed very important to her.

"Hmm." Mom grabbed another bag and slipped her items inside. "I'm not sure. Why?"

"Because, Mother." Ashley's mouth hung open. Five bags were piled up beside her on the assembly line. "Prizes are the most important thing." She lifted up the nearest bag. "These are nice, but I mean real prizes. For the winners."

"At our old school, the winners got medals." Kari placed another gel pen and small notebook in a bag and passed it to Erin. "Didn't you get a bunch of them, Ash?"

"I did." Ashley looked satisfied. "Medals would work."

"Medals aren't guaranteed, Ashley." Mom looked

at her. "Field Day is about having fun."

Ashley didn't look convinced. "Medals are better."

"Fine." Mom filled another bag. "What about you, Kari?"

"We learned about the meteor shower coming to Bloomington!" Kari glanced at Ashley and then Erin. "It's completely safe. Ms. Nan said so."

"Meteors raining down on us?" Ashley frowned. "I think I'll stay inside."

"No." Kari tried again to picture the stupendous event. "Meteors flashing across the sky. Like a light show."

Erin's eyes lit up. "I'd love to see that."

Mom nodded, impressed. "Sounds amazing. When is it?"

"Forty-one days." Kari felt her excitement leave. "But then . . . the worst part of the day was after lunch. Ms. Nan gave us a new assignment."

"What's that?" Mom was curious.

"We have to write a paper on what we want to do when we grow up." Kari let her hands fall to her lap. "But, the truth is, I don't know."

"I do." Erin's happy voice rang across the table. "I want to be a teacher!"

Ashley didn't hesitate either. "I'm going to be an artist."

"I'm doomed." Kari passed another bag to Erin. "I have no idea."

"Kari, it's okay." Mom smiled. "You can write about something that interests you. But you don't have to have all the answers. Not yet."

Just then, they heard the front door fly open and slam shut. Brooke rushed into the room, out of breath and teary-eyed. "My life is over." She tossed her backpack to the floor and dropped to an open seat at the table.

"Hello to you, too." Mom looked at Brooke. "Maybe you should tell us about it."

"Right. Hello, everyone." Brooke covered her face for a moment. "Sorry. It was the worst day."

Kari did not like when one of her siblings was upset. It made her stomach ache and her mouth dry.

Brooke looked around the table. "I have two tests and five assignments. All due this week. Plus,

Carly said she heard Stephanie Black tell Crystal Cummings that Donnie Baker is taking Stacy Campbell to the Fall Ball." Brooke was clearly out of breath. She took a quick gasp. "And Donnie is supposed to like me."

"Wow." Mom moved to the seat next to Brooke. "That's a lot, honey."

Brooke leaned her head on their mom's shoulder. "It's not like I even care about that. Donnie is immature. But I wish he would have at least asked me. I would have said no. But, like, it would have been nice. You know?" She took another quick breath.

Kari couldn't believe it. So much to deal with.

Their mother put her arm around Brooke. "I'm sorry, sweetheart. You're a little young for all that."

"No I am not. I'm not a child, Mom." Brooke pulled away. Tears spilled onto her cheeks. "Life is so hard!"

"Girls." Mom took a deep breath. She looked at Kari, Erin and Ashley. "Brooke and I need a little privacy." She smiled. "Maybe go join Luke out at the basketball hoop."

Kari and her sisters immediately jumped up and headed outside. Brooke didn't usually talk to Mom that way. In fact, no one in the family talked to their parents that way.

"I'm worried," Kari whispered to Ashley as they walked out.

Ashley shrugged. "Brooke's dramatic. The oldest, and all." Ashley clapped her hands. "Luke. Brooke's having a meltdown. Pass the ball." She waited for Luke to send it her way. "Come on! Let's have a game!" Ashley motioned to Kari and Erin. "All of us."

"No. We're missing Brooke." Kari crossed her arms. "I think I'll wait." She sat on the ground. Brooke had looked so sad. Distraught, even. If that was how people felt in middle school, then she never wanted to be there.

She would stay in sixth grade forever.

"I feel sad for Brooke." Erin took a shot from under the hoop. She missed. "Maybe we should make a card for her."

"We could clean her room." Ashley swished a shot from the foul line.

"Nice shot, Ash." Luke put his thumbs in the air. "Anything but cleaning."

"Ashley." Erin looked confused. "Brooke's room is always clean."

"Yes." Ashley smiled. "Exactly." She bounced the ball a few times.

"I have an idea . . ." Luke took the ball and tucked it under his arm. "We could get a dog!"

"Yes!" Erin gasped. "Great idea." She grinned at the others. "I've always wanted a dog."

Kari had stayed quiet on the bench. But she liked the idea of a dog. Especially for Brooke. Since she was getting older, and all.

"Kari, come play!" Erin waved her onto the court.

"Okay." Kari joined the others. "Brooke would love a dog. Before she gets too old."

"Yes." Luke waved his cast in the air. "She's almost a grown-up."

A few dribbles, and Kari threw a granny shot toward the hoop. *Swish!*

Kari pictured a dog out here with them. Brooke

31

by his side, petting him. Her smile relaxed. Yes, a dog would be the perfect way for Brooke to stay young. Now they just had to convince their parents about the idea.

Before Brooke got any older.

4

Field Day

ASHLEY

Ashley ate every bit of her scrambled eggs that morning. "Breakfast of champions," she told her mother. Then she pointed to herself. "Me, Mom. I'm the champion."

"I'm sure you will be." Her mother patted her head. "Get your shoes on. Can't win Field Day without shoes."

Her mom had a point.

Ashley sang a victory song as she finished getting ready. "I'm the winner of Field Day . . . no matter what my classmates say!"

Somehow she made it through the very long morning and lunchtime. And finally it was time for Field Day! The brisk, sunny October afternoon was perfect for an even more perfect day. She gathered with Natalie and the rest of her friends. "Come on." Ashley broke into a series of jumping jacks. "Winners warm up."

"Hey." Landon Blake came to her. "What are you doing?"

"Getting ready to beat you." She gave him a friendly smile. "No offense."

Landon laughed. "You'll be worn out before the first event."

"No." She did another three jumping jacks. "I'm going to be hyperfast before you take your first step, Landon Blake."

"Okay." Landon shrugged. "May the best runner win!"

They had already been placed on teams and in pairs, and Ashley was paired up with Natalie. Which was great news! Natalie was a true champion—at least on the inside. She found her friend. "Natalie. I need you to be on your A gate here. You get that, right?"

"A game." Natalie put her hand on Ashley's shoulder. "You've said that."

34

"Of course." Ashley jumped in place a few times. "Important things need to be said twice."

"You've said it four times." Natalie tied her tennis shoe laces. "Two more than twice."

"Four times, then." She really hoped Natalie was serious about Field Day. "Here are my final tips." Ashley lowered herself so she could look straight in Natalie's eyes. "Stay focused. Stay loose. Fight to the finish."

Natalie laced her other shoe. "You should be a coach."

"I am." Ashley stretched her right arm across her body and exhaled. "I'm coach of Field Day, Natalie. That's me."

"Keep in mind I've never done Field Day." Natalie stood and tightened her ponytail holder. "And I'm not very good at sports."

"Well, Natalie, think of it this way." Ashley took her hair band off her wrist and slipped it over her short hair. "Today is more like Feel Day. Cause of all the emotions." Ashley felt her bouncy ponytail. She was still getting used to her hair at this length. It had to be cut last month due to an unfortunate gum incident involving a certain student.

"Elliot!" Ashley called her friend over. "Come stretch with us."

He was flying his hand through the air. As if it were an actual spaceship. Plus he wore a cape around his neck. Elliot was one of the greatest people Ashley knew. He didn't care what anyone else thought about him. Also he was funny. And he was nice. Even if he had accidentally spit the biggest gumball into her hair a few weeks ago.

"Are you two ready for Field Day?" He swooshed his spaceship hand down and then spun in a circle.

"Yes." Natalie finished with her shoes. Finally. She stood and smiled at Elliot. "Are *you* ready?" Natalie pointed. "That cape might slow you down, I'm afraid."

"Don't worry, Natalie." Elliot stuck his chest out. "Capes make me run faster. But I won't be participating today."

"That's not fair!" Natalie crossed her arms.

"Elliot! You have to do Field Day." Ashley could feel her eyebrows raised very high on her face. "Why wouldn't you?"

36

Elliot shrugged. "Grass allergy. Any grass touches my skin, instant rash." He pointed at his sweatpants, tucked into white tube socks. "See? I made extra precautions today."

"Maybe you should watch from inside." Natalie looked worried about their friend.

"No." Elliot flung his cape. "I have to cheer on my friends. Good luck!"

"You're very brave." Ashley patted his shoulder. "Good luck to *you*." She shook his hand. "Watch out for flying grass, especially while I'm running." She did some high knees. "At my speed, grass flies everywhere."

"Thanks." He saluted her and then he ran off, his cape blowing in the wind.

Ashley raised her eyebrows at Natalie. "I like that Elliot. He's a good one."

Natalie pouted. "I wish I had a grass allergy. Then I could avoid this whole thing."

"Are you kidding me?" Ashley linked arms with Natalie. "I need my partner today!"

"I guess." Natalie exhaled. "Not like I really have a choice."

Just then Landon waved at her from the other side of the starting area. "Hey, Ashley." He was sitting by Chris. "I hope we can still be friends. You know . . . after I win."

Ashley squinted her eyes at him. "After *I* win, you mean."

Their PE teacher, Mr. Stone, raised a megaphone. "Attention, fifth-grade students. Please get to the starting line." Mr. Stone was bald. He had a mustache that covered a good part of his face and today he wore giant red sunglasses. He was funny that way.

Ashley spotted her mom on the other side of the field. "Hi!" Ashley waved big.

Her mom waved back and did a thumbs-up, as if she was saying, *You got this, Ashley!* It felt good to have a fan!

Ashley and Natalie walked to the starting line, along with the other students. Mr. Stone paced in front of them. "First, the Jump Rope Jubilee! Two students at a time. We'll count how many jumps you can do in a minute." He raised his hand. "Everyone line up."

A sick feeling began to grow in Ashley. She liked jumping. But jumping rope was a very different activity. Especially with everyone watching.

She and Natalie found a spot.

Mr. Stone blew the whistle and the first kids began to jump. Ashley twisted a little. Maybe Mr. Stone could give her a private location. Without so many eyeballs on her.

Before she could ask, it was her turn. She took her spot. *You can do it, Ashley,* she cheered for herself. *You can do it!*

"Don't mess up, Ashley Baxter!" The words came from mean Chris right before the whistle.

"Go!" Mr. Stone shouted.

Ashley began to turn the rope over her head. But on her third jump, the rope tangled up around her feet. She stopped and stepped free and then she started jumping again. Thirty-three jumps in a minute.

Terrible, she told herself. She handed the rope to the next person.

"Good job, Ash." Natalie patted Ashley on the back. When the Jump Rope Jubilee was over, Chris had won with seventy-three jumps. He flexed his arm muscles and gave everyone high fives.

Ashley was too busy drinking water to clap for him. Especially because of his rude words.

"Next up is the Water Bucket Relay," Mr. Stone shouted through the megaphone. "Boys versus girls." He explained that one teammate would grab a sopping wet sponge from the bucket at their feet, and then run it to an empty bucket. "You will then squeeze all the water out into the bucket and run it back to your teammate. First bucket to be filled, wins."

Ashley understood. "We can do this!" she yelled to the girls around her.

"On your mark, get set, go!" Mr. Stone blew his whistle and the teams set off.

Ashley cheered on each girl until it was her turn. She reached into the bucket and pulled out the dripping wet sponge.

"You got this!" Natalie shouted over the noise.

Across the field, Ashley could hear her mom cheering, too. Ashley took the wet sponge and ran it to the other end of the field. She squeezed the sponge into the bucket and ran it back. Amy was next. She ran off, her long braids swishing behind her.

Ashley leaned over on her knees, catching her breath.

"How do you feel?" Natalie hurried over to Ashley.

"Good." Ashley nodded. "Our bucket was way fuller."

"Yes!" Natalie ran off to share the good news. There were just a few students left to go.

Suddenly Mr. Stone raised his hand and blew his whistle. He was standing between the two buckets. "Girls win!" The girls huddled together and cheered, high-fiving and congratulating each other.

"Next up is the Marble Toe Grab!" Mr. Stone clapped his hands. "My personal favorite!"

Ashley froze. *What in the world?* She looked at Natalie. "Marble Toe Grab?"

Natalie frowned. "I really don't like this one."

She stared at her shoes and then at Ashley. "We have to sit barefoot on a chair in a kiddie swimming pool filled with marbles."

Ashley felt her eyes get bigger. She glanced down the field, and sure enough, there were two small blue and yellow plastic swimming pools with chairs at their centers. She turned to Natalie again. "Then what?"

"You have to use your toes." Natalie sounded disgusted.

Mr. Stone was saying how one person from each team would grab the marbles with their toes, and the other would catch them in a bucket.

Ashley raised her hand. "I'll do it." She took off one shoe and sock. "Natalie, you hold our bucket."

"Definitely." Natalie wrinkled her nose. "Too many germs in there."

Ashley didn't care. Their team was first up against Landon and Chris. Ashley sat on the plastic chair in the middle of the pool and pressed her feet into the sea of marbles.

"Wow!" Ashley yelled to her classmates. "This

feels like a marbley foot massage." She looked at Natalie. "You're really missing out here, friend."

Natalie rolled her eyes. She took hold of the bucket just as the whistle blew. From their separate kiddie pools, Ashley and Landon began grabbing marbles with their toes.

"Come on!" Chris held their bucket. "All the marbles you can get!"

Hurry, Ashley told herself. She picked up one shiny marble with her toes and moved it to the bucket. "One down!" She glanced at Landon and her heart dropped.

Landon was a professional marble toe-grabber, apparently. He had snagged four marbles, first try. One between each pair of toes. "We've got this." He grinned at Ashley. "You need bigger toes!"

"I like my small toes." Ashley tried for more marbles, but only one stuck.

Thirty seconds . . . twenty . . . ten. Mr. Stone blew the whistle again. Twenty-eight marbles for Landon and Chris. Six for Ashley and Natalie.

"The medal is ours!" Chris made a face at Ashley

and Natalie. He high-fived Landon. "Nobody has better toes than us!"

Ashley stared at the pool of marbles. *More practice*. That's what she needed.

Mr. Stone had his megaphone again. "Last event. The three-legged race!" Mr. Stone led the students to a bin full of red and blue bandannas.

"Here we go, Ashley. We have to win this one." Natalie sounded nervous. "We haven't won a single medal."

True, Ashley thought. And no medals meant she would no longer be Queen of Field Day. And that was a title she couldn't afford to lose, especially not at a new school.

Ashley focused. "Okay. Just like we practiced." She grabbed a bandanna from the bin and tied her ankle to Natalie's. "One step at a time. In sync."

"Right." Natalie nodded. "In sync."

Mr. Stone blew the whistle and three teams were off. Ashley saw her mom stand. "Come on, Ashley! You got this!"

This time her mother was right. Natalie and Ashley ran in perfect harmony, like they were born

44

for this very race. They crossed the finish line first and jumped around, hugging and shouting until the celebration landed them on the ground.

It didn't matter. Ashley and Natalie laughed and untied their ankles and hopped back up. "We won!" Natalie's happy eyes looked surprised. "We actually did it!"

After all the racers finished, Mr. Stone made the announcement. "The fastest score belongs to Ashley and Natalie! Congratulations, girls!"

And so their celebration continued. As they walked up to get their medals, Ashley looked at Landon. His Marble Toe Grab medal was already hanging around his neck. "Good job." She said the words very soft. So Chris wouldn't hear.

"You, too." He smiled and gave her a high five. Then he leaned in a little closer. "I knew you would win that last one. You're faster than Chris."

Ashley grinned. Yes, she was. She had beat Chris in a race last week at the high school football game. Mr. Stone placed medals around Ashley's and Natalie's necks. Ashley hurried over to Elliot. "Hey." She flicked his cape. "Did you stay out of the grass?"

"I did." He soared his spaceship hand around in the air again. "Plus I had more fun watching."

"I'm sorry about your grass allergy, Elliot." Ashley gave her friend a sad look. "Especially since winning is everything."

"No, it's not." He laughed and shook his head. "Winning *isn't* everything."

"What?" Ashley blinked a few times. "Are you kidding me here, Elliot?" She put her hands on her hips. "Winning definitely *is* everything."

"No, it's not." Elliot stopped soaring and smiled at her. "Lots of people don't win. I couldn't even play." He patted his own shoulder. "And I'm perfectly happy. Winning is fun. But it's not as fun as being happy or having a new friend or getting a good grade in reading." He fluffed out his cape. "It's not as fun as being yourself. I believe those things are more important, Ashley Baxter."

For a long time Ashley stood there. She looked at Elliot and then at her medal. Then back at her unlikely friend. And like sunshine after a cloudy day the truth came over her. It felt warm and new and wonderful. "You know something?"

Elliot waited. He was still smiling.

"Elliot, my friend." Ashley could hardly believe her next words. "I believe you're right."

On her way back to Natalie, Ashley thought of a bunch of things more important than winning. Working with her teammate and cheering on her classmates and seeing her mom across the field.

The truth was, she could be Queen of Field Day without a single medal.

But it was sort of fun having one.

That night before bed, Ashley drew a sketch of herself and Natalie running the three-legged race.

She drew medals around their necks and a few classmates cheering them on. Oh, and Elliot on the sideline, of course. In his cape.

Because the medal wouldn't matter after a week or so. But what Elliot had told her would last longer than that.

Maybe even forever.

5

Defense for a Dog

KARI

The fact that Kari hadn't stopped thinking about dogs all week told her two things. First, she really wanted one. Obviously. And second, it was up to her to convince her parents to buy one.

Brooke had come home frustrated every day that week, and also every day Kari found a way to talk about dogs.

"Mother?" she asked on Tuesday. "Did you know that people with dogs are happier?"

"How wonderful, Kari." Her mom didn't exactly look up from the kitchen sink, where she was working.

So Kari tried again on Wednesday. She sat next

to her mom during dinner. "Dogs can cheer a person up, Mother." Kari nodded at Brooke. "And someone in this family needs a little cheering. Don't you think?"

And on it went.

Now it was Friday and Kari had another plan. She had pasted magazine photos of dogs on a big piece of cardboard. She was in her room finishing the dog presentation when Ashley burst through the door.

"Dinner's ready." She flopped down on her bed and made a face. "Mom made salmon."

Kari put the exclamation mark at the end of her last bullet point and sat up on her knees. "I love salmon."

"Fish smell funny. They're better in the ocean." Ashley pointed to the board. "Impressive. A poster for your wall?"

"No." Kari laughed. "My case for a dog. Tonight's the night. For Mom and Dad."

Ashley hopped off the bed and studied the board. "This is amazing."

"Girls." Dad called from downstairs. "Dinner!"

"Okay." Ashley shrugged at Kari. "Let's do this."

Just before they got to the dining room, Kari set her dog presentation board in the hallway.

She took her seat and surveyed the room. She wasn't sure what approach to use. She didn't want to seem too eager, or too desperate. Then, she caught a look at Brooke, who was staring at her plate. She looked tired. Or sad.

That was it! Kari could be *really* sad.

Dad looked around the table and smiled. "Let's pray." He took Mom's hand on one side and Erin's on the other. Kari held on to Brooke's and Luke's hands, and Luke held Ashley's and Mom's. A perfect circle. Their family did this every night.

"God, we thank You for this family, for our friendship and health. Please bless this food and our time together. In Jesus' name, amen!" The family echoed with a round of amens.

"How was your day, honey?" Mom took a piece of salmon and turned to their dad.

He looked tired. "It was a tough one. A boy was admitted to the hospital with cancer. Alex Hutchins. I think he's a year older than Luke."

Brooke frowned. "That's terrible."

"Maybe we can help him?" Luke pushed his fork around in his broccoli.

Kari smiled at her little brother. Luke always wanted to help people.

"Actually there is something." Dad looked around the table. "The city is doing a 5K run in a few weeks to help raise money for Alex's medical bills."

"What time?" Mom nodded. "We could all participate."

Dad took a sip of water. "I'll find out."

"That's so sad . . . Sign me up, Dad. I'd like to help." Ashley ate a bite of fish. "On the plus side, I'm a very good runner. So possibly I could run extra . . . you know, to raise extra money."

"It doesn't work like that, Ash." Brooke took a sip of water.

"Brooke's right." Dad set his fork down. "For a 5K, runners get sponsors to donate and contribute. Also, the entry fees go toward the cause."

The conversation continued but Kari wasn't really paying attention. Her dog presentation was filling her whole mind.

Finally Mom noticed. "Kari, honey." She sounded concerned. "You've barely touched your fish. What's wrong?"

"I'm not too hungry." She picked at her dinner. "It's been a long week. Long month really."

Mom and Dad were watching her. Like they weren't entirely convinced.

Kari looked at her siblings, who seemed to be equally confused. Usually Ashley was the dramatic one. Kari sighed. "I'm supersad about the move, I think. And Ashley is very sad."

"I'm not sad!" Ashley dropped her fork and did a little dance in her chair. "I mean . . . I'm sad about Alex. But before that, I'm having the time of my life here and—"

"Fine." Kari held up her hand. "I'm not sad and I'm not sick. Sorry for lying." She took a bite of her salad. "I'm actually starving."

Ashley stopped dancing. "I was wondering about all that."

"Yes, well." Kari turned to her parents. She shook her head. "The truth is, I'm worried about Brooke. This has been the saddest week of our oldest sister's entire life. In case you've all missed it."

"Me?" Brooke froze for a few seconds. Then she looked at their parents. "I mean. I've had better weeks but . . ."

"Exactly." Kari would take what she could get. "Which brings me to the reason we're gathered here."

"Hmm." Dad grinned. "Dinner is what gathered us here."

"Hang on!" Kari ran from the room, grabbed her presentation board and rushed back. She held it up. "I present to you . . . my case for a dog." Kari walked the poster around the table. "Take a look, family. I think a dog is the answer to our problems."

"Problems?" Dad looked at Mom.

"Yes!" Luke shouted from the other end of the table. "Let's get a dog! Problems solved!"

Erin's eyes lit up. "Yes! A puppy!"

Kari liked where this was going. "See those puppy faces? They need us. See their eyes? They love us." She looked at her father. "A dog is man's best friend, Dad."

Dad sat back. "You don't say."

"I *do* say." Kari smiled. "And, Daddy, I haven't really seen you making new friends yet. A dog could fix that." *This is working,* Kari thought. "And think of Brooke."

"Kari . . ." Mom covered her mouth with her hand. She did a quiet little laugh. "This isn't the time."

Kari pleaded with her mother. "I'm almost done."

"Fine." Mom laughed again.

"Thank you." Kari had to hurry. Before they made her sit down again. "Not only is a dog a friend to everyone, but he's a great outdoor playmate. And . . ." Kari pointed to the poster. "A dog protects the whole family."

"Depends on the dog." Dad smiled. "A Chihuahua isn't much protection."

Everybody laughed at that.

"Plus." Erin raised both hands. "They're part of the family."

Kari smiled. "That, too."

Dad took a breath and sat forward. He placed

his forearms on the table. "Thank you, Kari. Can you sit back down, please?"

"Yes, I can." Kari set the poster in the hallway and returned to her seat. She took a bite of her salmon. It was delicious.

Dad looked around. "Dogs are a lot of work. They need to go on walks every day."

"I love walks." Brooke perked up. "I could help with that." For the first time all night, she seemed truly happy.

Dad nodded. "That's nice, Brooke. Thank you. But they also need to be fed."

"That's my job." Luke raised his hand.

Mom shook her head. "You're talking like we already have a dog." She looked at their dad. "What do you think, John?"

"Well, Kari." Dad looked at her. "I'm glad you were honest." He smiled. "Very impressive presentation." Dad clapped his hands together. "Maybe you should be a lawyer."

"Thank you." Kari took a bow. "Case dismissed."

• • •

The next morning, Kari was dreaming about puppies when she heard Dad's voice. "Kids. Get dressed." He sounded very chipper. "Mom and I have a surprise for you."

In record time Kari, Brooke, Ashley, Erin and Luke were up and at the breakfast table. Mom and Dad couldn't stop smiling, which Kari took as a good sign. Even still, none of the kids dared to guess.

Would this be the day? Was a puppy going to be theirs?

After they ate, they piled into the van and ten minutes later they parked in front of a building. The sign out front read: *Animal Adoption Agency*.

"Is this really happening?" Kari screamed. "We're getting a dog?" Kari unbuckled her seatbelt and leaned forward. "Are we, Dad? Are we?"

Dad turned off the car and looked back at Kari and her siblings. "Yes. We are." He laughed. "Your mother and I had already discussed it before we moved. And when you gave your presentation last night, we figured today was the perfect time."

"Plus it's fun." Erin grinned from the backseat.

"Sure." Dad winked at Erin. "That, too. We think you kids are ready for the challenge."

"Like what kind of challenge?" Kari leaned forward.

"Like feeding the dog twice a day. Walking it. Cleaning up after it." Dad nodded. "Are you up for the challenge?"

"Yes!" Brooke clasped her hands together.

Ashley nodded. "Yes. One hundred million percent yes."

"I'm in." Luke bounced a few times. "I'll do whatever it takes. Two thumbs up."

"I'm in, too!" Erin squealed, and Kari said the same thing.

"Let's go, then!" Dad shouted as they made their way into the building. "We decided to adopt a dog. A puppy without a home."

"Ms. Nan talked about that last week." Kari could hardly wait to get inside. "Lots of dogs need adopting."

Inside, they walked up and down several rows of dogs. Old dogs with white beards and young, hoppy dogs with extra energy. They saw tall dogs with spots and squatty dogs with wrinkles. At every cage, they stopped and said hello. But none of them seemed like the right one.

Until the very last cage.

There behind the bars was a brown furry puppy with big eyes and a waggy tail. He wasn't barking like some of the dogs and he wasn't crying like others. Kari thought the puppy almost seemed like he was smiling.

"Awww, he looks happy." Luke bent down. "Hello, boy! Do you like us?"

The puppy walked over and licked Luke's finger.

"I think that's a yes!" Dad lowered himself near Luke. He petted the puppy's cute head and then looked back at Kari. "What do you think?"

Kari's feet were dancing before she could answer. "Yes! He's our puppy! I love him already."

The others gathered around and Brooke looked at the sign on the cage. "It says his name is Bo!" She reached in and patted the puppy. "He's perfect. I feel happier already!"

Everyone laughed and the adoption worker

unlocked Bo's cage. "He's a sweet puppy." The girl didn't look much older than Brooke. "Golden retriever and Rhodesian ridgeback mix." She opened the cage door. "Someone left him on the side of the road. No family. No collar."

Kari's heart broke at that news. "Well, he has a family now!"

The worker put the puppy down. His tail swished back and forth while he went around the circle of Kari's family.

"It's like he already knows." Mom was last to pet the little dog. "He sure is cute."

"That settles it!" Dad swept the puppy into his arms and, after a few minutes of paperwork, Kari's family and their new pet were back in the van.

"He's so precious." Kari rubbed noses with their new dog. She and her siblings took turns holding the puppy on the way home.

Ashley put her face against his. "Bo Baxter!" She looked around. "What could be more perfect?"

Back at home everyone spent the rest of the day playing outside with Bo. But he was an inside dog, too. Dad and Mom said so. Which meant this was the actual best Saturday in the Baxter family history. The kids all agreed.

Before dinner Kari found her journal and turned to the first blank page.

I can't believe it! We have a new puppy!
He had a rough start. Someone left him
on the side of the road. And that's not
very nice because God made puppies to
be in families. Not in cages or on lonely
highways. But I'm not going to be sad
about Bo's old life. He's our dog now!

Which could only mean one thing: Kari's presentation had worked! The Baxters had a new puppy, Brooke had a reason to smile, and Dad had a best friend. But most of all their little brown dog would never be alone again.

Bo was home.

6

Last of the Toads

ASHLEY

Sunday school was almost over and Ashley was running out of time. She was painting a red barn for the top of Noah's Ark, something Noah should've done. Somewhere for the horses to sleep. One more brush of red across the side of the barn and it would be perfect.

In a rush, Ashley dabbed her paintbrush deep into the red jar, but she pulled it out too fast, and the jar tipped hard on its side. Red paint poured out like the flood in Noah's story. It flowed across the table and then over Ashley's painting of the Ark and the red barn.

It didn't stop there.

"Hey!" Natalie used a piece of paper to shield

her drawing of Noah and a pair of zebras from the red spill, but it was too late. "This was my best painting!"

"Yikes." Ashley spoke the word very softly. One simple mistake and the whole art table was on the edge of destruction. "I'm sorry, Natalie!"

Paint moved like a red river across the rest of Natalie's picture and then over Landon's drawing of what looked like a submarine-type ark. Landon laughed as his drawing disappeared in red. Clearly his picture wasn't the greatest loss of the moment.

"Someone, help!" Natalie grabbed a paper towel

and tried to wipe the red paint off her drawing, but it only made things worse. The more she wiped, the more her work disappeared.

"It's a real-life flood!" Ashley jumped around and waved her arms. "Teacher! Help!"

They had a substitute Sunday school teacher that day. *Substitute* meant the normally nice and helpful Miss Diane had been replaced by a girl who must not have known how to put paint in a flat dish.

Tall jars were never a good idea. At least around Ashley.

Suddenly the new teacher sprinted into action. She found a roll of paper towels and began wiping up the floodwaters of red.

"Sort of like the Red Sea." Ashley tried to sound hopeful. She pointed to the red-covered table. "This is perhaps the whole point of the story."

The new teacher gave her a glance. As if to say *perhaps not*.

Natalie was still cleaning up her painting and Landon was still laughing. He threw his artwork in the trash. Then he grinned at her. "You're the funniest girl I know, Ashley Baxter."

For a few seconds, Ashley didn't move. Didn't say anything. Because those words were not her favorite. Before she could say so, Landon was off with the other boys and Natalie held her red-covered painting up by the soggy corner. "A complete ruin." She dropped it in the trash.

It was time for Ashley to take responsibility for this Sunday school disaster. Something her mom and dad had always taught her. Accept the blame for your mistakes.

Some of the kids had already gone, but that didn't matter. She stood on the closest plastic chair. "Hello, everyone. I have an announcement."

Natalie and Landon looked at her.

Ashley crossed her arms. "I'm very sorry for the red sea on Noah's Ark day." She did a slight bow. "It was all my fault."

As she stepped off the chair, Landon clapped for her. Like this was, maybe, her best performance. "At least we'll remember the story."

On the way home, Ashley thought about Landon's comment. *You're the funniest girl I know.* What if she didn't want to be the funniest? Maybe she wanted to be the most talented girl or the prettiest girl. Or the smartest. Possibly the most unique.

She looked at her hands. They still had dried red paint on them. She was definitely unique. But *funny* meant people were laughing at her. All the time. Wherever she went. And right now that didn't feel very much like a compliment.

As they walked into the house, Ashley caught up with her dad. "Do you think everyone expects me to be a disaster? First at school and now at church?" She had already told her parents about the red paint flood.

Dad put his arm around her shoulders. "No, honey. Not at all."

Ashley nodded. "You think they're surprised, then? When I'm a disaster? Each time it happens?"

"You're not a disaster, Ashley. You're perfect just the way you are." He kissed the top of her head. "Don't forget that."

"Thank you." Her daddy always knew what to say. Even so, there was just one thing she wanted to do now that they were home.

Ashley ran up to her room, washed her hands

in her bathroom and found her art supplies. Down in the kitchen, her three sisters were helping Mom with brunch. Ashley stepped up to her mother. "I don't believe my kitchen skills will add anything to the meal this morning." She held up her sketchbook and colored pencils. "May I have a pass to the outdoors?"

"Yes, Ash." Mom patted her shoulder. "You can do cleanup."

She headed out back with Bo. This would be her first drawing of the new puppy. But as Ashley sat on the bench next to the big tree, Bo began to run around the yard, bouncing and hopping and sprinting every which way.

Like he was having his own personal Field Day.

This was a problem. Bo had to sit still if she was going to draw him.

"Bo!" Ashley tried to whistle. "Come here!"

He was chasing a fly, trying to catch it in his mouth as it flew around his nose.

"Yoo-hoo! Bo!" Ashley snapped her fingers a couple of times. "Sit, Bo."

The fly flew away, so Bo sniffed the grass. Then

he found a leaf. Ashley gave up. If the puppy wasn't going to sit still she would have to guess a little. She started with his paws and legs and then his body.

"Hmm." Ashley studied her sketch. Bo's legs were much too long and his paws looked huge. Maybe she could bring it all together when she drew his face.

"Bo, a little help over here, please." If only she could get a steady look at his eyes and nose. "Come on, boy!"

Finally, Bo stopped sniffing and running and looked at her. He tilted his head to one side, and then the other. Ashley moved her pencil over the paper as fast as she could. She was about to draw his ears when Luke stepped onto the back porch with his basketball.

He dribbled it a few times, and in a flash Bo was off.

Bo liked hoops, apparently.

"Luke! I was drawing him!" Ashley was on her feet. "Send him back."

"Sorry!" Her brother jogged to the basketball hoop near the garage. "Bo! Go back to Ashley!"

Instead the puppy ran three circles around Luke. Her brother shrugged. "He said he wants to play."

Ashley dropped back to the bench and stared at her drawing. "Fine." She added the ears and studied her work again. Extra-long legs, gigantic feet, long droopy ears halfway to the ground. A crooked, happy smile.

This Bo looked more like an alien. Something Elliot might find on one of his pretend adventures to Mars. She closed her sketchbook and scowled.

Dark clouds gathered in her brain. This day was turning from bad to very bad. Bo had barked and cried all night, which meant almost no sleep. Then there was the red paint flood, and now she'd drawn the worst-looking dog in the history of drawing.

Her frustrated thoughts grew louder as the day played out.

Brooke was too busy with homework to join Ashley, her siblings and Bo at their giant rock near the stream at the back of the house. Brooke had never missed a meeting at the rock. "I'm growing up." Brooke shrugged. "It'll happen to all of you one day."

And that night when they walked into the house for dinner, the whole place smelled like dirty socks.

Ashley plugged her nose as she took her spot at the table. "Who has their shoes off?"

"Hey." Her dad sat down and grinned. "That's your mother's dinner. She made my favorite. Beef stroganoff and creamed spinach."

"Wonderful." Ashley leaned back in her chair. "The worst food in the history of the world." She raised her hands and let them fall on her lap. "Why would anyone want that?" Her siblings were all in place around the table. "Well? People? Tell me you agree here."

Silence. Not one of her sisters . . . not even Luke

agreed with her. They had all teamed up against her, and now she was on an island of not liking the dinner choice all by herself.

"Here we are!" Mom walked in with a casserole dish and set it on the table. She had a proud look on her face. "The perfect dinner."

Ashley stared at the goopy mess. Apparently her mother hadn't heard her comments. "May I have a pass please?"

Mom settled into her seat and gave Ashley a funny look. "A pass?"

"Yes. A pass." In the corner of her eye, Ashley saw her dad take a deep breath. *Think fast,* she told herself. "A bathroom pass . . . A hall pass . . . You know . . . a way out. That sort of thing." She looked once more around the table for support. Again there was none. Her eyes found Mom. "So . . . yes. A pass. Please."

Dad set his napkin down a little harder than usual. "There is no way out, Ashley. No pass tonight. And please be kind. Mom worked very hard on this dinner."

No one understood her. "I'm trying to be kind."

Ashley's thoughts buzzed around in her brain like flies at a summer picnic. "I'm just hopeful that maybe I can sit this one out." That was something Brooke sometimes said when they played a family kickball game. *I'll sit this one out,* she would say. And she would get a pass to the sidelines.

But there was none of that for Ashley tonight.

Mom seemed to finally understand that her dinner was the problem. "You don't like beef stroganoff and creamed spinach, Ash?"

Ashley blinked a few times. "Do you?" She fanned the air near her face. "That smell . . . like the trash can after—".

"That's enough." Dad was very serious. "No more complaining, Ashley." He looked at the others. "Let's thank God for our food."

After the prayer Dad smiled at their mother. "Tell us about your day, my love."

"Well . . ." She put her hand over her mouth, the way she sometimes did when she was trying not to laugh. "I spent the last few hours cooking."

Everyone was taking big sloopy scoops of the dinner, which only stirred up the smell and made the room feel heavy. Like the smelly food was moving through the actual air now.

Ashley took a small bit of the dish and tried to breathe through her mouth.

"Hey!" Erin raised her fork in the air. "I really like this dinner!" She grinned at their mom. "We haven't had it in years."

"It's been a long time." Mom smiled. "Thank you, Erin."

That did it. Ashley crossed her arms and stared at her plate. This was the worst day. She had failed at Sunday school art, failed at drawing Bo, and now her whole family had turned on her.

Kari chimed in next, telling Mom how great the dinner was . . . as if beef stroganoff and creamed spinach was better than pizza. Brooke was eating her plateful just fine, and so was Luke.

Only Ashley was the outsider.

"Ashley." Her mom handed her a piece of bread from the basket at the middle of the table. "Here." Kindness warmed her mother's eyes. "You don't have to eat the dinner. Not everyone has to like it. I understand."

The first good bit of news all day! Her mom understood. Ashley took the bread and slathered it with more butter than usual. Tears stung her eyes as she took a bite. The rest of dinner she looked only at her bread. Not at her family or the yucky dinner or Mom's nice eyes.

Better to keep to herself. Before something else happened.

After dinner, Luke cleared his plate and announced that he was going out back to catch toads. "Unless they're gone for the fall."

Brooke went to the front room to read her history book and the other girls followed Luke outside. Dad, too.

Only Mom stayed. "Would you like more bread?"

Ashley shook her head. "I don't want this piece, actually."

"I didn't think so." Mom moved to the spot next to Ashley. "Not the best day, huh?"

"Everyone thinks I'm a disaster. They laugh at me and don't stick up for me and sometimes they leave me out." Ashley's eyes grew watery. "Plus I think I've lost my skills as an artist, Mother. You should see my terrible drawing of Bo." She rested her forehead on the table for a few seconds and then she sat straight again. "Everything in my head is sad."

Mom took hold of Ashley's hand. "Thoughts can be like that."

"Yes. My thoughts are all grouchy and frustrated."

"Hmm." Mom was quiet for a minute. "Sometimes thoughts are like autumn toads. Hard to catch."

Ashley looked at her mother. "What do you mean?"

"The Bible says we should think about what's good and true. Beautiful things and things we admire." Mom's voice was kind. "When sad thoughts fill our hearts, we can talk about them, of course. But eventually we should think about happier things instead. It's our choice."

"So we can catch the sad thoughts and tell them to leave?" Ashley sniffed. "And then instead think about happy thoughts?"

"Yes." Mom patted Ashley's hand. "Happy thoughts are always just a think away."

"A think away." Ashley smiled. "I like that." Just then Bo ran in from outside and came right to Ashley's feet. He licked her bare ankle and panted. Like he wanted to play. Ashley giggled. "Like thinking about a brand-new puppy?"

"Exactly." Mom took a long breath. "There's so much to be thankful for, Ashley. And the truth is no one believes you're a disaster. People laugh *with* you, because you're funny in a good way. And the only reason your brother and sisters didn't stand up for you today is they didn't want to make *me* feel bad."

Ashley nodded a few times. "I can see that." She made a face. "It really was a terrible dinner. Just being honest."

"You're not the only one who has disaster days. That dinner smelled awful." Mom laughed out loud. "And between you and me it tasted worse."

"You don't like stroganoff?" Ashley was shocked.

Mom giggled and shook her head. "No. But your dad loves it. So I make it for him."

Now they were both laughing, and suddenly Ashley understood what Mom meant. She could mope around thinking upsetting thoughts and believing the worst about the people she loved. Or the dinner she'd made. Or she could remember the truth . . . that her family loved her and she loved them. And even if Ashley was prone to disasters, Mom was right. People weren't laughing at her. Not even Landon Blake. They were laughing *with* her. That was a better way to look at things.

Just then Luke ran in with the biggest toad cupped in his hands. "I did it! I caught one!"

Ashley smiled.

Because she had just done the same thing.

7

Animals and Dancing Queens

KARI

Exotic Animal Day had finally arrived for Ms. Nan's class. But as Kari walked down the hall to her classroom, she wondered if one of the animals had escaped. Maybe a boa constrictor or an iguana or a bear. Something must've gotten loose because students were bunched up near the classroom door.

Kari pushed her way through the sea of people. Turned out the kids weren't looking at a loose animal. They were staring at a sign-up sheet for the school's talent show. Kari's stomach dropped, like when she rode that roller coaster last spring.

A few girls signed their names to the sheet, and then three boys from her class did the same thing.

A talent show? Kari grabbed the straps of her backpack. She had never done anything like that before. Kari spotted Mandy and Liza. She waved them over.

"Look!" Kari pointed to the sign-up sheet. "A talent show! The three of us are loaded with talent!" She looked at her friends. "I think we could win the whole thing!"

"Hmm." Mandy's eyes looked nervous. "What would we do?"

"I'm not sure. Juggling, maybe?" Kari tried to imagine that. She could feel her excitement building. "Or maybe singing?"

"No." Liza wrinkled her nose. "I would be too nervous."

"But you *love* singing!" They needed to sign up before all the spots were taken.

"Not in front of people." Liza shook her head. "No talent show for me, Kari. I'm too scared."

The bell rang. Kari had to act fast. She quick grabbed the pen that hung next to the piece of paper and she signed up Liza, Mandy and herself.

"Hey!" Liza's mouth hung open. "I said no!"

"And I was about to." Mandy looked like she might faint. "What if we have no talent?"

"We do!" Kari linked arms with her friends and hurried them into the classroom. "I'm great at finding talent! You'll see."

Kari's mind raced as they took their seats. She had told the truth. She had seen talent in Ashley long before her sister started gymnastics. And she had been absolutely sure Brooke would do great on her tests in middle school.

She was a born cheerleader! That's what her mom always said. Surely she'd find some sort of talent for the three girls before the show. For now she couldn't think about that.

Because lined up on a long table at the front of the classroom were four large cages covered with blankets. Each of them held a different zoo animal. Surprise zoo animals. Like possibly a baby lion or a small rhino or a long-toothed baboon. If there were such a thing.

Kari wasn't sure.

But she was glad her desk was in the second row and not the first.

Their teacher stood a few feet from the animals. Next to her were two zoo workers: a tall skinny man with gray hair, and a pretty girl with a blond ponytail and a friendly smile.

Ms. Nan clapped her hands. "All right, class. Today we begin learning about different careers. My goal is to help you explore options so you'll choose something to write about. Ideas for when you grow up."

Kari stared at her shoes. Right. This again. She hadn't thought about the growing up assignment since the day it was introduced. Kari felt her heart beat harder. After a few seconds, the palms of her hands grew sweaty.

She didn't want to think about this. Not today. Her brain was busy enough thinking about the talent show.

Ms. Nan continued. "We begin the exploration of future careers today by looking at the life of a zoo employee and learning about exotic animals!" The class didn't make a sound. Ms. Nan smiled. "Thank you ahead of time for paying attention to our zoo friends."

The tall skinny man traded places with Ms. Nan. "My name is Anderson." He motioned to the other worker. "This is Kristen."

Kristen waved. "We work at the Indianapolis Zoo!"

Anderson pointed to the row of cages. "The animals we brought today are very friendly. But try your best to keep quiet. And please no sudden movements." He hesitated. "Kristen. Can you bring out our first friend?"

Kristen stepped up to the first cage and removed the blanket to reveal a porcupine. The class gasped and some kids in the front row backed up. Kari winced. She'd heard about dangerous porcupines. Throwing spiky things everywhere. She didn't trust them.

"This is Pork." Kristen smiled. "He is a porcupine. Pork uses his strong feet and curved claws to climb trees." She touched the animal's feet. As if she wasn't afraid at all. Then she moved her hand just over Pork's back. "A porcupine is covered with sharp spines called quills. And some porcupines have up to thirty thousand of them on their body!"

Kari glanced at the classroom door. If quills started flying she was ready.

The other zoo worker took over. "Some of you may wonder if porcupines can shoot their quills. They actually cannot. No need to worry."

Best news all day, Kari thought to herself.

By then, Kristen had Pork in her arms. She walked him around the room and when she passed Kari's desk, Liza screamed. "This one can shoot his quills. I can see it on his face!"

Kari agreed. The porcupine definitely looked ready to attack. She covered her face with her hands and peered through her fingers. No matter the danger, seeing Pork this close up was a thrill.

Anderson stepped forward while Kristen put Pork away. The zoo worker picked up a superlong boa constrictor from the next cage. Several of the students screamed and ran to the back of the room. Mandy moved closer to the front and Kari stayed at her desk, her hands near her face again.

After the boa, Kristen showed them an opossum and Anderson brought out a bearcat. Which was the same as having a real-live bear in the classroom. Kari joined Liza at the back of the room for that one.

Kari was pretty sure she wouldn't work at a zoo when she grew up. Mandy, though, stayed at the front of the room until the presentation was over. Liza whispered close to Kari. "If Mandy runs a zoo someday, you and I can visit her."

"Definitely." Kari could picture that. "Someone has to buy tickets."

During lunch, Kari, Mandy and Liza sat at their usual table. Kari ignored her lunch and leaned closer to her friends. "I have ideas about the talent show."

"I told you." Mandy crossed her arms. "We don't have talent."

"Not much, anyway." Liza shook her head. "I'm not ready for the stage."

"Well, my friends." Kari grinned at them. "We'll just see about that."

. . .

A sleepover was the best choice to get their talent figured out. Kari had set the event up with her mom and now it was Friday night and Mandy and Liza were in her living room. Ashley sat nearby reading *Peter Pan*, while Mandy read from a list they had been making all week.

The list of their potential talents.

"Juggling. What about that?" Kari tapped the pen on her cheek and looked at Mandy and Liza. "If we worked on it, maybe?"

"Definitely not." Mandy waved her hand in the air. "I drop my pen four times a day. I know I couldn't juggle."

Ashley looked up from her book. "Is jungling with coconuts?"

"What?" Liza blinked a few times. "Why coconuts?"

"Because." Ashley set her book down. "Jungle. Jungling. That's where coconuts live."

Kari understood her sister. "Not *jungling*, Ash. *Juggling*. It has nothing to do with the jungle."

A wrinkle crossed Ashley's forehead. "I picture it in the jungle."

"Either way, that's not our talent." Liza stood and paced to the front window. "We should drop out, Kari. We have no talent."

Mandy raised her hand straight in the air. "I know!" She stood and began swimming her arms through the air. "We could do a swim team dance."

"Creative!" Mom walked in with a bowl of popcorn. She set it down and put her hands on her hips. "You would definitely be the only swim team dancers in the talent show."

"Hey!" Kari was on her feet. She pulled Liza off the sofa and swung her over to Mandy. "A dance! That's what we'll do! A group dance!"

"Hmm." Liza had the popcorn bowl. She set it down on the coffee table. "That could be fun!"

"I usually just swim dance." Mandy dropped to the floor and sat cross-legged. "But there's something no one knows." A huge smile filled her face. "Secretly, I love to *regular* dance. I think it's my hidden talent."

"Perfect!" Kari swung her hands from side to

side and snapped her fingers. "I told you I was good at finding talent!" She walked over to her parents' radio and turned it on. The music that poured out was "Under the Sea" from the movie *Little Mermaid*. The tune sounded upbeat and fun.

"Come on!" Kari pulled her friends to the center of the living room. "Let's dance!" All three girls linked arms and moved their feet. They were not a well-oiled machine, but Kari believed there was hope.

Mom sang out from the kitchen. "I love this song! Come on, Ash!" Their mother hurried into the living room with a towel on her shoulder and a spoon in one hand. She helped Ashley to her feet and twirled her around.

They made a dancing train. Kari, Liza and Mandy followed Ashley and Mom around the house as the music blared from the speakers. "Plus," Kari yelled over the song, "this is about being under the sea!"

Mandy seemed to catch on. "Which is sort of like swim dancing!"

"Exactly." Kari kicked her feet even higher.

"The words are pretty fun." Liza didn't look

as convinced as the others, but she was happy. Another good sign.

When the song ended, Mom ran off to her bedroom. She came back with a cassette tape. "I have the movie soundtrack right here!" She handed it to Kari. "'Under the Sea' is the sixth song."

Kari held the tape high in the air and danced it over to her friends. "So are we in? We'll do a dance to 'Under the Sea'?"

Mandy didn't hesitate. "I'm in. We should definitely include swim strokes." She swam her hands out in front of her a few times.

"Hmm." Kari remembered to smile. Mandy looked like she was digging at an invisible pile of dirt. "Very nice, Mandy. We'll think about that."

The decision was Liza's now. Kari and Mandy stared at her. "Come on!" Mandy was fully on board. "Liza, you'll be the best dancer in the group!"

Liza seemed to hold her breath for a few seconds. Finally she grinned. "Okay! Let's do it!"

For the next hour, Kari and her friends played the *Little Mermaid* song over and over and over again. The dance moves they decided on came mostly from Kari, but Ashley and their mom created a few, too.

By the time the girls went to sleep, the dance was half finished. Kari could hardly contain her excitement. They weren't only going to have a wonderful act for the talent show.

They were going to win the whole thing.

8

The Play and the Pet Fairy

ASHLEY

Ashley sat on the floor with her classmates while Mr. Garrett read *Peter Pan* out loud. Every word had a grip on Ashley's heart. Already they had read about Peter, the Pirates, and the Lost Boys.

But Ashley was most like Wendy.

The oldest Darling sibling loved pretending things and she was always ready for an adventure. Also, Wendy was nice to her brothers. Ashley thought Wendy's trek from London to Neverland was a lot like Ashley's journey from Ann Arbor to Bloomington.

Only with less pixie dust and more smelly gas stations.

No doubt, Ashley and Wendy would've been best friends.

Mr. Garrett kept reading. They were at the part where Peter had come to realize that the Lost Boys and Wendy had been captured by Captain Hook. As Peter sets out to rescue the crew, Tinker Bell realizes something.

Hook is trying to destroy Peter Pan.

So Tinker Bell risks her own life to save Peter. And now, her light is fading.

Ashley felt tears at the corners of her eyes. Poor Tinker Bell. But Tink's act of kindness made Ashley proud of the little fairy.

Tinker Bell had done the right thing for Peter Pan.

"Peter swore this terrible oath." Mr. Garrett was nearly done with the chapter. "Hook or me this time." He shut the book and looked at the class.

"Is he gonna take down Hook?" Chris sat near Mr. Garrett's feet. He hadn't blinked once during the whole chapter. "Is Pan gonna give him what he deserves?"

Mr. Garrett set the book down. "We'll have to wait and see."

Ashley raised her hand. "Mr. Garrett?"

"Yes?" Their teacher looked at her.

"Now. I know Tinker Bell is a fairy." She twirled a piece of her short hair. "But I was thinking maybe we should get one. You know, for the class."

Mr. Garrett pressed his lips together and squinted. "A class fairy?"

"Exactly. Hear me out." Ashley sat up on her knees. "We had a pet last year at my old school. A butterfly." She bounced a little. "So, maybe we could get a pet in the form of a fairy."

"Ashley." Her teacher shook his head. "Fairies are pretend. You can't . . . go to the store and buy one."

"What?" Ashley couldn't believe this. "Where is your faith, Mr. Garrett? Your trust?"

"And where's your *pixie dust*?" Chris made a face at her. A few of the kids laughed.

Ashley stared at him. "At home. In my top dresser drawer." She smiled at Chris. "I'm guessing you don't have any pixie dust, Chris. Because you don't believe."

"You do not have pixie dust at home because—" Chris was louder now.

"Yes, I do!" Ashley was on her feet. Mean Chris was not going to win this conversation. "I have pixie dust because I got it from my dad for my birthday. It came in stick form."

"No, you didn't." Chris stood, too. The whole class was watching. "That's candy, silly!"

"That's enough." Mr. Garrett moved closer. "Ashley, there are no fairies. No pixie dust." He gave a stern nod. Then perhaps as an afterthought, he smiled. "Though it's very fun to pretend."

Ashley was disappointed in Mr. Garrett. "We should at least try to find a class fairy. In case they're real." She looked around.

Only Natalie and Elliot had the slightest hope in their eyes.

"Fine." Ashley did a slight nod at Mr. Garrett. "I will make it my personal project to find a class fairy. My family has the exact sort of yard for that."

Their teacher sighed. "Okay, Ashley. I won't try to stop you. But fairies are definitely not real."

Elliot cried out and collapsed to the ground. For a few seconds he lay there, eyes closed, arms and

93

legs sprawled out. Ashley giggled. Elliot was a lot like Peter Pan.

"Elliot?" Mr. Garrett rushed over to him. "Are you—"

"I'm fine." Elliot sprang back up. "But the fairies are not fine, Mr. Garrett. That's what happens to a fairy every time you don't believe." He raised both hands in the air. "The book told us that."

Mr. Garrett laughed. He asked everyone to take their seats. "I have good news, boys and girls. Our class is doing a skit for the talent show. The story of Peter Pan in ten minutes." He opened a large box near his desk. Inside were piles of wigs, costumes, swords and wands. "At this time, I will assign a role to each student."

Natalie raised her hand. "No thank you, Mr. Garrett." She shook her head. "I'm camera shy."

Ashley stared at her friend and whispered, "You're shy of the camera?"

"No," she whispered in Ashley's direction. "I'm shy of the public."

"This assignment will help you, Natalie." Mr. Garrett grabbed a stack of papers from his desk and began handing them out, along with props and costumes. He looked back at Natalie. "Doing something out of our comfort zone helps us learn new skills."

What part would she get? Ashley held her breath. It had to be Wendy. She actually was Wendy!

"Hook, for you, Mr. Blake." Their teacher gave Landon a fake hook, a bushy black wig and a pointy pirate hat.

Landon slipped on the hook. "Sweet!" He swiped it toward Chris. "Arrrgh! Ahoy, mateys!"

Ashley studied her friend. Landon was an intimidating Hook. But Chris would have been better, since he had the personality of a pirate.

"What do I get to be?" Chris took a packet from their teacher.

Mr. Garrett handed Chris a teddy bear. "You are Michael Darling."

Chris frowned. "The baby?" He crossed his arms. "I don't wanna be the baby."

Perfect, Ashley thought. She covered her smile with her hand. From the back of the class she heard laughter from a few kids.

"He's not a baby. He's just . . . little." Mr. Garrett gave Chris a thumbs-up. "You'll be great."

Chris took hold of the teddy bear. He looked like he might drop it on the floor. "I wanted to be a pirate."

Mr. Garrett kept walking. "Amy. You will be Tiger Lily, the native warrior princess of Neverland. She is also our narrator." Their teacher handed Amy a flower crown.

Amy placed the crown on her head. "I always wanted to be a warrior princess!"

"Miss Baxter." Mr. Garrett handed Ashley her packet.

Ashley gasped. She couldn't believe what she saw. *ASHLEY BAXTER—WENDY*. Her prop was a necklace with an acorn on it. Like the one Peter Pan gave Wendy in the story. Peter called it a kiss. It was her kiss necklace. She looked up. "Are you sure?"

"I am." Her teacher smiled. "You'll be the perfect Wendy."

"Thank you." Ashley stood, arms wide. "You're right. I already am the best Wendy, Mr. Garrett. I won't even have to act for this part."

Mr. Garrett laughed. "I'm glad you're happy." He raised his eyebrows. "You can sit back down now, Ashley."

"Yes, sir." Ashley stared at the acorn necklace. She was more than happy. Mr. Garrett could have given the part to someone who wore dresses all the time, like Natalie. Or someone with perfect hair, like Amy. Instead he saw what Ashley had seen a long time ago.

She and Wendy were practically twins.

"Elliot." Mr. Garrett gave Ashley's friend his part along with a green hat and red feather. "No debate about it. You *are* Peter Pan."

Elliot stood and saluted. "It is an honor to play the boy who never grows up as I, myself, have aspirations of doing the same. I won't let you down!" He crowed a few times, a wild rooster crow, like Peter had done in the book. The class gave Elliot a round of applause.

"Natalie." Mr. Garrett gave out her role last. "I chose you as Tinker Bell." He handed her the packet and a bag of glitter. He held one hand up alongside his mouth like he had a secret. "Don't worry, she doesn't have any lines."

"Congrats!" Ashley gave her friend a high five.

Natalie sighed. "I hope I'm not on stage much. I am so happy I don't have any lines." She thumbed through the packet a bit.

"Also, you'll probably get a pretty costume, and wings!" Ashley was trying to highlight the good since Natalie truly was stage shy. "Plus. You'll be with Elliot or me the whole time basically. So this is the best of both words."

"Worlds." Natalie still looked nervous.

"Worlds?" Ashley blinked.

"Yes." Natalie giggled a little. "It's supposed to be the *best of both worlds*. Not *words*."

"Hmm." Ashley shrugged. "Seems like if it's the best of Elliot or me it's the best of both words." She thought about that. "Elliot. Me. Two words. But whatever you say."

Mr. Garrett was back at the front of the room. "We will start on our class play tomorrow. Our show will include some lines, and narrating, and then two songs from the Disney film. I will bring the music in tomorrow. I passed out the props so you would know what belonged to you. But for now, let's put them in the box and go back to our desks for a little bit of math!"

When Ashley got to the box, she held on to the kiss necklace for a few seconds before putting it back. She wanted to savor the feeling of it in her hand. "Thank you, Mr. Garrett. Come on, Tink, let's fly to our desks!" She tapped Natalie and the two of them fluttered off back to their chairs.

Math could definitely use some pixie dust.

As Mr. Garrett and the class moved on to fractions, Ashley had a thought that she hadn't had before. Maybe she didn't need a class pet fairy after all. Because she had the best version of a fairy anyone could ask for in her new best friend, Natalie. The real-life Tinker Bell. Who, by the way, had real-life pixie dust.

And that was better than any class pet fairy she could ever find.

9

Talent Show Tryouts

KARI

After days of dancing under the sea in the living room, Kari believed they were finally ready for tomorrow's audition. It wasn't a real audition, Mom had read off the handout they took home. Because no one would be cut from the show for lack of talent. But if the "talent" wasn't ready or the act wasn't safe or appropriate for school, then the teachers in charge could use their adult powers to decline the act.

So, today, Kari was determined to make sure she and her friends weren't booted from the program. Which was why she danced her way through the afternoon to Mom's cassette as she waited for Mandy and Liza to arrive for their last practice.

They needed every move to be perfect.

"Kari." Brooke sat on the couch. She was doing homework again. "You don't have to worry. You're a great dancer. They're not going to cut you."

Kari spun around and kicked her leg in time with the music. "How do you know that, Brooke?" She lifted her arms to the sides and did a half turn to the beat. "What if we're not ready?"

"You are." Brooke set her pencil down.

Erin lay on the floor, chin on her hands, watching. "I think you're perfect. A superstar!"

Brooke agreed with Erin. "You're well rehearsed. You have no live animals. And you're not doing anything that crosses lines."

Ashley walked into the room. "Crossing lines?" She plopped onto the sofa. "Is that like jumping fences?"

"Exactly." Brooke smiled. "You aren't jumping fences, either."

For a few seconds Ashley took in Kari's dance moves. "I say you're an ideal act for a talent show."

"I say so, too." Erin sat up, cross-legged. "Dance it again. I'm trying to learn it."

Kari paused the music and put her hands over her head to catch her breath. "I hope you're right." She paced a bit. "I can't forget the steps tomorrow. I just can't."

Brooke closed her textbook and stood. "Here's what you do." She sucked in her cheeks, clasped her hands together and shot them straight in front of her. Then she pretended to swim herself from one side of the living room to the other.

Kari laughed. "You want me to be a fish?"

"Why not?" Brooke stopped swimming. "Your song is 'Under the Sea,' right? If you forget your moves, just swim around onstage."

"Yeah." Ashley nodded. "People will think that's part of the show!"

Erin chuckled as well and rolled around the floor. "You could do this, like a sea urchin!"

Pretty soon they were all laughing. Then all of a sudden Brooke gasped. "You need a costume!"

Kari sat on the arm of the sofa. "Liza's mom is making us green sequined tops."

"I know!" Ashley jumped a few times. "Mermaid tails! That's the perfect costume for 'Under the Sea'!"

Brooke put her hands on her hips. "Ashley. Can you imagine dancing in a mermaid tail?"

"No one would know if they made a mistake." Ashley grinned. Then she started to laugh. "I guess that wouldn't work too good."

"Too well." Brooke sat back down and opened her book. "Grammar is important in middle school."

"Yes, well." Ashley dropped to the floor next to Erin. "I'm going to pass on middle school. Like Peter Pan."

"I like that." Kari loved her sisters. Never a dull moment. "Middle school does seem like a lot of learning."

Brooke blew at a wisp of her hair. "You have no idea."

"Ladies and gentlemen." Luke came running down the stairs and into the living room.

Kari laughed. "Just ladies in here, Luke."

"Fine." He held his arms out to his sides. "Ladies and ladies . . . I present to you . . . Your dancing queens!" He flicked the lights off and pulled a flashlight from behind his back, which he aimed at Kari. "Doing their original performance of 'Under the Sea'!"

"Luke, what are you doing?"

"Your group needs a name and an announcer." He turned the lights on again and set the flashlight down. "I'd like to join your act!"

"Dancing Queens?" Kari nodded. "I like it. Dancing Queens under the sea!"

"Sounds famous." Ashley looked at Luke. "When did you get so smart?"

"Mom said I was born that way." Luke smiled big. "Actually, I have basketball practice that night, so I can't do the show with you. But I really think you should be the Dancing Queens."

With that, he ran off to the kitchen.

Liza and Mandy arrived then, and by dinnertime Kari was sure they had two things: a dance routine and a group name. But the Dancing Queens needed one more thing to pull off their audition.

Courage.

The next day after school Kari sat with Liza and Mandy in the auditorium watching the auditions. With every act that took the stage, Kari felt a little more nervous. Maybe they shouldn't have signed up. They could've supported the other kids and just enjoyed the show. What if she tripped walking up there? What if she forgot the moves and fainted? What if—

Terrible possibilities did a different kind of dance in Kari's brain.

Kari turned and saw Mom at the back of the auditorium. She waved and mouthed, *You can do this!* Kari's nerves calmed down some. Having Mom here was a big help.

Miss Patty, the school's music teacher, was in charge of the auditions. She held a clipboard in her hand and took lots of notes. Sometimes she sat, and other times she stood, or walked back and forth. A large pair of eyeglasses were perched on her head and she fidgeted with the string of beads that hung around her neck.

A boy named Mac was performing now. His act was called "Mac the Magician." So far it wasn't going so well. His face was red and he was trying another trick. "And out of thin air . . ." Mac tried to pull what looked like red flowers out of his sleeve. Only the flowers got caught and he yanked them too hard. Then with a loud *ZZIPPP*, his entire sleeve fell to the stage.

Mac stared at his sleeve. Then he gave Miss Patty a nervous smile. "No sleeve! And for my next trick . . ." He picked up a wand and a glass of water from his small table. He balanced the glass on the tip of his wand and held it straight in front of him.

The audience of people waiting to audition burst into applause. Which must've startled Mac, because at about the same time the water spilled toward him and soaked his T-shirt. He did a short laugh. He was still smiling.

Good for you, Kari wanted to tell him. *Don't give up, Mac!*

Now he was trying to juggle oranges. Instead he sort of threw three oranges in the air and watched them crash to the floor. So instead of putting on an exciting magic show, Mac was drenched, with a missing sleeve, chasing oranges around the stage.

Kari thought that maybe he should've been a comedian.

Mac removed his top hat and took a bow. His routine was over.

"Well . . ." Miss Patty nodded a few times. "Maybe rethink some of these tricks, Mac. I would suggest no water glass. But good try." She sighed and gave him a thumbs-up. "Next please."

Mac collected his things and hurried offstage. Kari watched his friends high-five him and pat his back. Like he was the greatest magician of all time.

Relax, Kari told herself. *Miss Patty is clearly an understanding judge.*

Next came a perky girl named Darlene. She wore a bright red curly wig, a white dress and tap shoes. "Hello. I'm Darlene. I will perform a piece from the Broadway musical *Annie*." She clicked her toes on the floor and did a little shuffle step. "The sun will come out, tomorrow . . . bet your bottom dollar that tomorrow, there'll be sun!"

Darlene's dance moves were impressive. Plus Kari liked the song. Although Darlene's voice didn't quite match the notes, Miss Patty seemed impressed. Darlene hit the last note and struck a pose, hands raised, nose in the air.

She was already a star!

"Great, Darlene." Miss Patty clapped and then

jotted something on her clipboard. "Thank you."

The next act was the one right before Kari and the girls. A boy walked onstage with no props. No special shoes. No costume pieces. Just himself. He spoke with a monotone voice. Almost like he was half asleep. "Hi. I'm Tyson. And I am going to do some of my sounds." He cleared his throat.

The room was quiet. A high-pitched noise blasted through the speakers for a second, which caused everyone to cover their ears. Another teacher ran over to the soundboard and messed with some of the knobs. It was silent again.

Someone in the back coughed.

"Okay. Here we go." Tyson cleared his throat again. *"Ooooowaout!"* He scooped his voice from low to high. *"Heeeeshaw!"* Somehow, his voice got higher. *"Bleech! Blaach!"* This time it sounded like he was coughing.

Kari squinted her eyes. She wasn't convinced that this was a talent. She exchanged looks with Liza and Mandy. They all tried their best not to laugh. Mandy had to cover her mouth. It wasn't that they were laughing *at* Tyson. But the sounds were so silly.

Which maybe was a talent.

He finished with a final *"Wompawindah!"* A loud shout that echoed through the whole theater. Then, he stepped forward, bowed and left the stage.

Kari wasn't sure if Tyson's sound act would make the show. But Tyson had done his best and given everyone a few minutes of laughter. So there was that.

Miss Patty slumped into a chair at the front of the stage. Her smile looked tired. "Thank you . . . Tyson. For your . . . creativity." She looked at her clipboard. "Last, but not least, we have the three Dancing Queens. Kari, Liza and Mandy."

Kari took a deep breath. *Help me remember the moves, God.* She handed one of the parent volunteers the tape with "Under the Sea".

Mandy linked arms with Kari. "I'm nervous."

"It's just the audition." Liza didn't look scared at all. "We have time."

As they reached the top of the stairs, Kari turned to the girls and grabbed their hands. "Let's have fun!" They got in their positions. Kari gave the parent volunteer a head nod and the music began.

The song started and ended in a blur of dance

moves. Despite a few slipups, Kari thought they'd done a fantastic job. Miss Patty stood and clapped. "Bravo! You Dancing Queen girls are great. Keep practicing."

Liza and Mandy and Kari hugged each other and hurried down the stairs and off the stage.

"Great job, everyone. See you at swimming later." Mandy waved as she headed off to where her dad waited for her.

Liza left with both her parents and Kari ran to her mother. "We did it!"

Her mom hugged her. "You really are a dancing queen!"

"Thanks for being here." Kari slipped her backpack on. "You're the best."

Mom ran her hand over Kari's head. "Of course! I wouldn't miss it. Your dad would be here, but he's helping Luke and Erin with homework."

"I know." Kari smiled. "Plus, they'll all be at the talent show."

"They will." Mom spun around. "Kari . . . you know you got your moves from me, right?" Mom twirled again. "Under the sea . . . under the sea . . ."

She kept singing the song, which made Kari laugh. By the time they reached the parking lot, they were both singing and dancing.

Kari was thankful for a lot of things. But especially her mom. Someone who was there for her no matter what. Whether she and the girls would've ripped their sleeves or tripped over themselves and landed on the floor, her mother would be here. Always.

Because that's what moms do.

10

Lost in the Corn Maze

ASHLEY

Late October was Ashley's happiest time because it meant three things: Mom baked more. The trees were dressed in their best yellows, reds and oranges. And this year Ashley's class was taking a field trip to the pumpkin patch.

It was Sunday afternoon and Mom was baking again. In the last week she'd made pies and muffins, scones and cookies. Every day the house smelled like brown sugar and warm cinnamon. This afternoon it was apple oat bars. The mixture of sweet spiced apples with the crunchy oat topping was Ashley's most loved snack.

Ashley sat on the back porch and stared at the tree a few steps away. She had her sketchbook and pencils. The sun was going down so the light was perfect. Golden hour, her dad called it. Also Ashley loved autumn leaves. The sort of living masterpiece only God could paint.

With little strokes, she began to bring the colors to life. Most of the leaves were on the ground now. Soon they'd all be there, which made Ashley a little sad.

She wished autumn could last forever.

A leaf wiggled on the closest branch. "Don't fall!" Ashley whispered. "Hang on, little leaf." A gust of wind blew across the yard and the leaf left the tree and swirled toward the grass.

Ashley dropped her art supplies and chased the leaf as it floated on the wind. Just when she thought she would never catch it, the wind stopped and the leaf landed in her hand. "Wow!" She studied the colors and the lines. "You're the most beautiful leaf in the whole world."

She placed it in her sweater pocket, careful to not ruin it.

Sitting back down with her drawing, Ashley took a quick look at her picture and smiled. It was one of her favorites. The pretty tree, leaves dancing to the ground. Also a little bench near the trunk where she drew herself with her sketchbook.

Sometimes it was fun to put herself in the drawing.

The air got colder and Ashley joined her family for dinner. Everyone went around the table and said what they liked most about the day. Brooke was glad for no homework and Kari was happy about Mom's apple oat bars. Erin was thankful for time with their family and Luke was excited about training Bo to sit.

"What about you, Ashley?" Dad smiled at her. "I bet you're happy about your drawing. It's one of your best."

"Yes." Ashley tapped her fingers on the table. So many good options. "That's a nice one. But I think my very favorite is that today is one day closer to tomorrow."

Her family waited a few seconds and then Kari giggled. "What's that mean?"

"It means . . ." Ashley stood and spread her arms out to her sides. "Tomorrow is our class trip to the pumpkin patch! And today . . . is one day closer." Ashley pointed at her mother. "Also Mom is going to chaperone!"

Everyone was happy for Ashley, and after dinner she counted the hours till bedtime.

Finally it was Monday morning and Ashley felt buzzy about the fact. With everything in her, she knew it was going to be the best pumpkin patch day ever!

• • •

The school bus pulled up to Bloomington's Blossom Farm and the students and chaperones all piled out. The bus happened to park right next to a puddle.

"Please step *over* the muddy water," Mr. Garrett shouted more than once.

Even still Elliot plopped right into it. Water sprayed everywhere, and two of the chaperones screamed. But Elliot just laughed, like maybe he preferred muddy shoes on a pumpkin patch day.

Ashley understood. Mud was a pretty fun situation.

On the way to the ticket booth, Mom walked with Ashley. "That boy who jumped in the puddle . . . is he a troublemaker?"

"No." Ashley shook her head. A thought hit her. "Elliot is a . . . trouble-*faker*."

Mom took Ashley's hand in hers. "I haven't heard of that."

"Well. It's when someone likes to be goofy and make people laugh." She looked back at Elliot. He was jumping along while the other kids walked. Ashley raised her eyebrows at her mother. "Adults might think he's making trouble. But he's only faking, Mother. You know, to be included in the jokes and stuff."

"Ashley's right." Suddenly Landon Blake was walking with them. "Elliot's had some low moments. Like when he blew gum into Ashley's hair." Landon winked at Ashley. "But he's a good friend."

Then Ashley remembered. Her mother didn't know this unlikely friend! Ashley pointed at him. "This is Landon Blake." She cupped her hands around her mouth and whispered toward her mother. "I thought he was a menace. But he's fine. I checked."

"Landon! Come look at the hogs!" Chris shouted from a ways ahead.

"See you later, Ashley." Landon jogged off toward Chris. He looked back. "Nice to meet you, Mrs. Baxter."

"Bye." Ashley watched Landon go. She turned to her mom. "He's the boy who won the other half of the medals at Field Day."

"I see." Her mother smiled. "He seems nice."

"Yes." Ashley smiled. "He's one of my unlikely friends."

Once they were past the gates, the kids broke into groups. Everyone had to be back at the barn for lunch, which gave them three hours to explore. Ashley's group had Natalie and Elliot and Chris and Landon.

The tractor hayride was first for their group. Ashley and her friends climbed onto the trailer behind the tractor and found seats on bales of hay. Ashley's mom sat in the middle between Ashley and Natalie.

"Mrs. Baxter." Natalie grinned at Ashley's mother as the tractor set off across the field. "I'm glad I'm in your group."

"Because . . ." Ashley kissed her mother's cheek. "You, Mom, are the chaperone extraordinaire."

They passed five cows and Elliot began making mooing sounds.

"Elliot!" Ashley tapped his shoulder. "Cows don't like people pretending to be in the flock."

"Really?" Chris gave her a funny look. "A flock of cows?"

"Yes." Ashley tried to stand but the tractor hit a bump and she crashed back to the hay bale. "*Flock* means lots, Chris. Lots of cows, of course."

Natalie gave Ashley a nervous look. Then she whispered, "Herd. It's a herd, Ashley."

Mom winced and gave her a little nod. Her face said Natalie was right.

Ashley did a small cough and stared around Natalie to Chris. "*Flock* herd. That's what I'm saying. Cows flock in their herd."

Elliot mooed again and Ashley responded with a moo of her own. The others did the same, but not like Ashley and Elliot. They were the best mooers in Mr. Garrett's class.

The tractor sputtered up a grassy hill where they had a view of the whole farm, including the goat pen and the corn maze. Then as they passed a coop of chickens, a huge field of pumpkins came into view.

They stopped and Ashley's group scampered off the trailer. Ashley ran ahead of her mother. She zigzagged through the patch, jumping over vines and examining each pumpkin. "I know you're here, perfect pumpkin!" She skipped over another vine. "Where are you?"

Just then Mom held out a pumpkin. "Here! Ashley, look!" It was perfectly round and had the best stem in all the patch.

Ashley squealed. "I love it." She grabbed the pumpkin and hugged it. "I will name him Clancy."

Her mother brushed her hands on her jeans. "That's a nice name."

"Thank you." Ashley held Clancy the pumpkin tight. "Just so you know . . . I'm having the best day with you today." She hugged her Mom's waist.

"So am I, sweetheart." Mom held Ashley tight. "So am I."

The group decided on the corn maze next. Only Mom stayed back with a few of the chaperones. Everyone except Natalie was excited to make their way through the maze. Natalie was worried about her radiant red rain boots. That's what she called them.

They were partway through the confusing trail when Elliot stopped. "Um. I think we made a wrong turn." He was definitely trying to sound brave. But his knees were shaking. He sneezed. "Plus I think this corn is getting the best of my allergies."

"We should've brought my mom." Ashley tossed her hands. "Now we'll live the rest of our lives out here in this maze."

"I told you this was a bad idea." Natalie stared at her new boots. They were brown now, covered in mud. "My boots are ruined!"

"Well what did you think they were for?" Elliot wiped his nose with his sleeve.

Natalie crossed her arms. "I thought they were for being cute."

Landon and Chris had gotten ahead of them, so it was just Ashley, Natalie and Elliot now. Ashley stood between Natalie and Elliot. "Stop! We won't find civilization by fighting about rain boots!"

At that exact moment a loud shout came at them through the corn. *"BOO!"* Chris jumped through the stalks onto the path next to them. Ashley, Natalie and Elliot all dropped to the ground at the same time. Ashley and Natalie screamed.

"Gotcha!" Chris doubled over laughing. "I got you all good!"

Elliot picked himself up off the ground. Mud

clumps stuck to his chin, and he sneezed again. "That's not funny, Chris."

"It was pretty funny." Chris peered into the corn. "Landon! Come out here!"

Landon came out seconds later. He looked embarrassed. "Sorry. We . . . didn't really mean to scare you."

"Yes we did!" Chris was still laughing. "Landon, you should have seen it. They all fell to the ground."

The expression on Landon's face looked angry. "Quit it, Chris. That's not nice." He walked over and helped brush the mud off Elliot's face. "It's only funny if no one falls."

Chris actually seemed to think about that. His shoulders sank. "I guess you're right." He helped brush mud off Natalie's rain boots. "Sorry."

Ashley wiped a few mud smears from her knees. Then she looked at her two messy friends. "Should we take a vote?"

"For what?" Elliot's eyes were getting red.

"Whether we should accept Chris's apology." Ashley raised her chin and stared down her classmate.

A slight smile lifted Natalie's lips as she looked at Chris. "Yes." Natalie nodded. "*We* accept your apology."

"I accept it, also." Elliot was really sneezing now. If they didn't find their way back to the real world soon, he would melt into the mud.

"Me, too." Ashley shook Chris's hand. "Don't let it happen again." She felt a shiver of concern. "Either of you two know the way out? I don't want to live here forever."

"Follow me." Landon took Ashley's hand and the two of them ran ahead. "Lunch is in ten minutes. Come on!"

Sure enough, Landon knew the way. He only held her hand for a minute, since they really weren't that lost after all.

When they stepped into freedom, Landon grinned at her. "I'd never let you live forever in that corn maze."

A warm feeling spread through Ashley's heart. She did a slight curtsy. "Well, thank you." The group of them began running for the barn. Ashley shot Landon one more glance. "And I would never win all the Field Day medals. A few really did belong to you."

At lunch, Ashley told her mother about getting lost and nearly not surviving the corn maze. And something else. How Landon Blake was a mystery. A jokester and a rival and a friend. All at the same time.

Which was why she shared her ride home with someone she could truly count on.

Clancy, the pumpkin.

11

The 5K Day

KARI

Today was the day of Alex Hutchins's 5K run.

All morning Kari couldn't get her mind off of Alex and how unfair it seemed that he was sick at the hospital with cancer. She hoped today would be a big success and, if everything went well, a lot of money could be raised for the Hutchins family. Dad said the money would go to Alex's medical costs, like treatments and procedures.

"When a child is sick, the whole family struggles," Dad had told them. Kari thought that was sad but the good news was this: The whole community wanted to help. This morning, Mom and Dad were even letting them bring Bo.

Since four-legged runners were welcome, too.

Kari looked out the van window as they pulled into Town Square. Downtown Bloomington bustled with traffic, and Main Street was lined with tents displaying fruit and vegetables and baked goods for sale. Corn hole and horseshoes were set up on one stretch of grass and music played from a nearby speaker. People of all ages and sizes stood in groups—talking, stretching and getting ready to run. They all wore paper numbers across their shirts.

Bo bounced around, barking and smiling. Like this was the best way to spend a Saturday morning. Dad held Bo's leash. He petted their dog's head and helped him calm down. Then Dad and Bo led the way to the registration table.

Luke was the last of the family to sign up. "I always wanted to run a marathon!" He grinned at Mom, who stood nearby with the rest of the family.

"This isn't a marathon." Brooke patted Luke's head. "A marathon is twenty-six miles. This is five kilometers." She smiled at him. "About three miles. I learned that in school."

Kari and the others stepped up to the next table, where a happy lady with a long red braid and a white visor gave them each a paper number. "Here you go!" She handed Kari the number 54 and two safety pins. "Attach this to your shirt. I'm glad you and your family are joining us."

As Mom and Dad helped them with their numbers, Kari looked back at the woman with the red braid. Did she know Alex? Or was she just helping out? Dad said Alex's family would be here today. They must be happy so many people had come out to support Alex.

The Baxter family found a section of grass and Ashley lay on the ground to stretch. Kari dropped down beside her. "You ready?"

"No." Ashley grunted. "First the corn maze . . . now this. All in one week. It's a lot on a person."

Luke, who was doing jumping jacks, chimed in. "You'd feel better if you hadn't gotten lost in the corn maze."

"That was five days ago." Mom laughed. "I think Ashley has fully recovered."

"You'd be surprised, Mother." Ashley rolled her

eyes at their little brother. "Plus, we weren't only *lost*, Luke. We were miles from civilization." She reached for her toes and held that position. "We were thinking about surviving on corn. Forever."

Kari giggled at Ashley. Every time she told it, her story grew worse. She patted Ashley's shoulder. "Don't worry. Dad said we don't have to run today. We can walk if we're tired."

"Right." Brooke held her arms out and moved them in little circles. "We just have to finish."

Luke ran in place a few times and held his arms straight up. "And I . . . plan to finish first!"

"Luke . . ." Erin sat cross-legged on the ground. "There are adults here. Professionals." Just then a group of runners walked by. They wore tight-fitting runner outfits, with sleek shoes and matching water bottles. Erin giggled. "See. Those kind of people are going to win this thing."

Kari watched her mom and dad talk to a man who was probably Alex's father. The man looked happy and sad at the same time. After a while, Kari's parents joined the family again. Bo looked ready for the race, because he wasn't barking now.

"It's almost time." Dad clapped his hands.

"I'm going to win." Luke started doing jumping jacks again. "I'm practically a professional." He was already out of breath. "Right, Dad?"

"One day you might be." Dad ran his hand over Luke's hair. "Second grade is very young to be a professional runner." He grinned at each of them. "Today let's just do our best."

Alex's dad stepped onto a platform and took hold of the microphone. "First, thank you for showing up today." His eyes looked damp. "I . . . can't believe you would all come out to run and walk for my boy."

Kari and her siblings stood a little closer to Mom and Dad and Bo. *Being sick must be very hard*, Kari thought. She looked up as her mom leaned her head on Dad's shoulder. Mom whispered, "It makes me thankful for our health."

Kari realized how important it was to be here for Alex. There were lots of ways to show someone you cared. Bringing dinner or making a card for someone who was sick. Today this was the best thing they could do for Alex and his family.

"Some of you have asked about Alex." From his spot on the platform, his father looked at the crowd. "Alex is in the hospital today. He . . . needs a miracle." The man seemed to wipe a tear from his face. "And today you are a part of that miracle."

Next to Kari, Erin hugged Mom's waist. "We need to keep praying for Alex."

Mom's eyes looked watery. "Yes." She kissed the top of Erin's head. "We can do that."

A different man took over for Alex's dad and told everyone that their registration fees from the race had raised fifteen thousand dollars for Alex's family. Then he talked about the rules. "Stay on the path, don't turn around and please pick up after your furry runner friends!"

Bo gave a single bark and everyone laughed. "Good boy." Dad patted Bo's head. "You're going to love this!"

Kari and her family moved closer to the starting line. Dad had his arms around Mom and Kari. "Mr. Hutchins asked if we could swing by the hospital after the race. To see Alex and cheer him up." Dad nodded. "I said we would."

Ashley skipped up alongside Kari. "I can tell him a joke!" She did a twirl. "I'm an absolute riot, you know."

Luke raised his hand. "I'll show him my basketball cards!"

Mom smiled. "Perfect."

Kari thought for a minute. What could she do to cheer up Alex? Maybe bring in her music and do the Dancing Queen routine for him? Or talk about her swim team? No, that wouldn't work. Alex was only a year older than Luke. He wouldn't care about swim team yet.

Then an idea hit. Kari could tell him about the meteor shower! Yes, Alex would love that!

"Attention, runners and walkers." A voice came over the speaker. "The race will begin in five minutes!"

"Kari." Ashley looked very serious. She leaned in close and whispered. "I don't want to scare the younger children. But . . . I don't think we have enough food."

"What?" Kari blinked. "We're supposed to be running. There won't be time to eat."

"For five days?" Ashley shook her head. "I thought Mom and Dad would be more prepared. We don't have tents or sleeping bags. Plus it's practically freezing out here." She rubbed her arms. "I know it's for Alex. But a *five-day*? I didn't train for this."

"Ashley." Kari stared at her sister. "You think it's a five-day race?"

"Yes! Dad said so." Ashley put her hands on her hips. "What do you think a *five-day* means? We run for five days. Straight. No breaks." She slumped over. "I'm already exhausted."

Kari tried not to laugh. "It's not a five-day race, Ash." She put her hands on her sister's shoulders. "It's a *5K*!"

"Five *K*s? What does that even mean?" Ashley stood straight again. "Walking in a K pattern five times? How long does that take?"

Brooke must have been listening because she chimed in. "The *K* stands for *kilometers*. It's a way to measure distance." She blew at a wisp of her hair. "Things you learn in middle school! Weren't you listening? I *just* said this a bit ago." Brooke laughed.

"I must have missed it." Ashley looked relieved.

Dad and Bo walked up. The whole family gathered around. "What's happening?"

Kari grinned. "Ashley thought the race lasted five days straight." She put her arm around her sister. "She thought it was a *five-day*."

"Oh, honey." Dad still had hold of Bo's leash. "I'm sorry. You should have asked us about that. If we run some and walk some, it'll take less than an hour."

Ashley bent over her knees and did a loud sigh. "Whew!" She wiped the back of her hand across her forehead. "Thank you for clearing that up. I can breathe a little better now."

"Three miles is still a lot." Erin looked to the starting line. "But we can do it!"

"Okay." Dad waved everyone close. "Baxter family huddle!" He looked at each of their faces. "Remember, it's not about winning." He winked at Luke. "This is for Alex. So pray for him . . . think about him as you run or walk. Let's try to stay together."

"Because together is more fun!" Kari smiled at her family.

"Exactly." Mom grinned.

"Hands in!" Dad put his hand out and everyone stacked their hands on top of his. "One . . . Two . . . Three."

"Team!" The whole family shouted the word at the same time.

Moments later, a buzzer sounded and the race began.

Kari and her family stayed mostly at a slow jogging pace. Halfway through the run, they stopped at a water table. Volunteers even had water bowls for dogs, so Bo got a drink, too.

"Okay . . . let's walk a bit till we catch our breath." Dad looked at Mom and the kids. "Then we can run again at the end."

Walking will be good, Kari thought. Her feet hurt and she was sweaty. But she didn't complain. At least she wasn't like Alex, in the hospital fighting a sickness.

When the finish line was a block ahead, Luke and Dad and Bo began to run. Fast. Brooke and Erin kept at a walking pace, and Kari and Ashley and Mom jogged.

Ashley clapped her hands. "We can do this!" An older couple ran past them, and Ashley called out. "Keep up the good work!"

They smiled back at Ashley and waved.

One by one, the Baxters crossed the finish line. They each got another cup of water and then they headed back to the van. On the way, Mom bought a bag of apples from one of the vendors.

Halfway home, with Bo asleep on the seat beside her, Kari stared out the window. She couldn't stop thinking about Alex in the hospital. "Mom?" Kari turned to her mother. "Why do some people get sick?"

"Well . . ." Mom thought for a long time. Like she was trying to make sense of that question herself. "Sometimes sad things happen. It's not heaven . . . so people get sick or hurt."

Brooke and Ashley and Erin and Luke were listening, too. Like maybe all of them also wondered why Alex was sick.

Dad looked in the rearview mirror at all of them. "I think God is just as sad as we are when bad things happen."

Kari liked the idea of that. She pictured God standing with people in their sadness and sick times. She looked at Mom again. "Because He loves us, right?"

"He does." Mom took their dad's hand. "So very much."

Kari gazed out the window again. The sky had turned gray, and rain clouds were moving closer. That meant somewhere, God was sad today, too. Sad for kids like Alex and all the broken arms and broken hearts. In that moment, Kari felt like she understood more of who God was.

And that made her smile.

They dropped Bo off at home and drove to the hospital. Alex's dad met them in the lobby. "Alex needs to rest soon. But he doesn't have brothers and sisters. So he'd love to meet you all."

The man led the way up the elevator and down a hall to Alex's room. It was full of balloons and get-well-soon cards.

Alex sat up and smiled. Three thin tubes were attached to his arms, and his bed was surrounded by beeping machines. His head looked bald but it was hard to tell because he wore a baseball cap.

"Hi, Dr. Baxter!" Alex didn't sound sick. His eyes lit up as he looked at Kari's dad. "You brought your family!" He waved at Luke. "Hey . . . I remember you!"

"I'm Luke." He took a step closer. "We played kickball together."

"Before I got sick." Alex grinned even bigger. "Don't worry. I'm getting better. I'll be on your team when I get back to school."

"Okay." Luke took hold of the railing that ran along Alex's bed. "I'll save you a spot."

"Wow, Luke." Alex looked at Kari and her sisters. "You're the only boy!"

"It's not that bad." Luke smiled back at the girls. "Sisters are a lot of fun, actually."

Luke showed Alex his basketball cards, and the boys spread them across Alex's hospital blanket.

"Alex." Ashley stepped up. "You should know I'm the original Wendy. From *Peter Pan*."

Alex looked surprised. "Really?"

Dad gave Ashley a look. "Well, not—"

"Father." Ashley's eyes grew shocked. "You cannot

deny the fact. Mr. Garrett named me Wendy. And I'm very original." She turned to Alex again. "So I'm the original Wendy."

"That's cool." Alex laughed. "I always wanted to meet Wendy."

"And now you have." Ashley bowed. "Alex, why was the broom late?"

"Why?" Alex hesitated. Like he wasn't sure where this was going. Ashley had that effect on people.

"Because . . ." Ashley held out both arms. "The broom overswept!" She glanced around. "Get it, people? It over*swept*! Instead of *overslept*."

Everyone laughed. They were all relaxed, like they could have been at home in the living room.

"Okay! That's enough." Dad raised his eyebrows at Ashley. "Alex needs his rest."

"But, Dad, I didn't get to the—"

"That's all, Ashley." He chuckled and put his hand on Alex's shoulder. "How are you feeling, Alex?"

"Better now." He grinned at their dad and then Mom and the rest of the family. "Thanks for coming here."

"We'll be back!" Ashley gave Alex a high five.

Brooke and Erin told Alex they'd be praying for him. If Kari was going to say something to Alex, this was her moment. She moved in by his bed, right next to Luke. "Hey, Alex, did you know there's a meteor shower coming to Bloomington in two weeks? It's like a shower of shooting stars."

"My dad and I talked about meteor showers last year!" Alex sat a little taller in his bed. "I've always wanted to see one."

"Me, too." Kari liked Alex. He reminded her of Luke. "I learned about it in class. We're gonna watch it at our house. You should come." By then, Alex would probably feel better. He could come to the house and play basketball with Luke and help Mom bake. And then he could hang out with the family and watch the sky show. Since he didn't have brothers and sisters.

Kari thought it was the perfect plan.

"I'll ask my parents!" Alex blinked a few times. "It sounds fun!" He yawned and leaned back in his bed.

Dad patted Alex's foot. "We'll let you sleep, buddy. See you soon."

They all said their goodbyes and on the way back to the lobby, Alex's dad thanked them. "That was so good for him." He looked at Mom and Dad. "Keep praying."

"We won't stop." Dad shook the man's hand.

Later that night, as Mom and Dad made dinner, Kari sat on the couch with her journal. She had some thoughts about today, thoughts she didn't want to forget.

Today we had fun at the 5K. We raised money for Alex and his family. Then we visited him in the hospital. I don't even know him, but he's a lot like Luke. And, God . . . I know you're sad that Alex is sick. So if You could please make him better in time for the meteor shower. That would be the best. Dinner's almost ready. Gotta go! Love, Kari.
P.S. 14 Days until the Meteor Shower!

Kari closed her journal and looked at Ashley, sitting beside her sketching. "What are you drawing?"

140

"Alex at the finish line." She smiled at Kari. "Instead of in the hospital."

"Oh." Kari nodded. "That's nice." She looked at Ashley and a hundred memories came rushing in. Days on Lake Monroe and times at the rock at the back of their yard. Everyone in her family was here and not at the hospital.

And that made Kari so thankful.

Ashley stopped drawing and turned to Kari. "Why are you staring at me?"

"I don't know." Kari smiled and shrugged. "I'm

just thankful." And she was. She loved her life. She loved her family. And she loved her home. She loved that everyone was happy and healthy and she never wanted that to change.

Not in a million years.

12

The Rowdy Rehearsal

ASHLEY

Ashley juggled her book in one hand and a flashlight in the other. She wasn't totally sure what time it was. Kari was asleep across the room and the rest of the house was quiet. Ashley had no choice but to keep reading.

Mr. Garrett said they had to finish reading *Peter Pan* by tomorrow. Ashley had two chapters left. She'd meant to finish it yesterday morning. But they had the 5K—which thankfully was not a five-day race.

Ashley turned the page. *Peter Pan* was her favorite book of all time. She peered at the window. Maybe this was the day Peter Pan would show up. Because Ashley was Wendy. So one day he would come here and together they would fly by the second star to the right and off to Neverland. Brooke and Ashley, Erin and Luke would have to come, too, of course.

Then they could swim with the mermaids and teach the Lost Boys how to bake. And together they would fight the pirates and—

She remembered the book. *Focus, Ashley! Keep reading!*

This part of the story was where Wendy and her brothers were headed back home to the nursery on Hook's boat, captained by Peter Pan himself. But instead of sailing on the high seas, they were flying on the clouds, back to London.

Ashley kept reading. When the children arrived home, Wendy's parents were asleep. They had been so worried for their kids that their father, George, had been sleeping in the doghouse.

Imagine that, Ashley thought. *Dad sleeping in Bo's doghouse.* The picture made her giggle. Suddenly a drawing filled her mind. She shut the pages of *Peter Pan* and reached for her sketchbook.

Before she forgot.

She drew Dad sleeping on the floor next to Bo—since Bo didn't have a doghouse. And just outside the window, Ashley drew herself. Because being Wendy would be fun, but the end of the story was best of all.

Being home at last.

At school the next day, Mr. Garrett's class was deep in rehearsal again, and Ashley was about to walk the plank. Which was the scariest part of being Wendy. She held her breath and waited.

The desks in Mr. Garrett's class were pushed to

the back of the room, and everyone was running through the play one last time before the talent show.

"I'll get you, Pan!" Landon swiped his hook in the air and Elliot ducked. The hooky hand barely missed him.

"Not today, Hook!" Elliot pointed to the sky.

Landon took a deep breath. "We'll see about that!" He looked mean. Not like the usual Landon Blake at all. "I'm going to tie up Wendy!"

He came to Ashley with a short piece of rope. They didn't have an actual pole like a real pirate ship. But Ashley could see the pole anyway. Landon took her hands behind her back and tied them together.

"Not too tight." Mr. Garrett sat on the edge of his desk watching.

"Okay." Landon gave Ashley a quick grin. "Don't be scared," he whispered. Then very loud he said, "She's *my* prisoner!"

Ashley almost missed her next line. She remembered to pretend. "Never!" Fear filled her voice. "Peter, help me!"

Chris stood next to Ashley. He held his teddy bear and he sounded bored. "Oh no, Wendy. Are we going to have to walk the plank?"

"Hold." Mr. Garrett stepped forward. "Chris. You're supposed to be frightened. The script says he is crying. You're the baby."

"I am not!" Chris shouted back, defensive.

"Not *really* a baby. But you're playing one. It's make-believe." Mr. Garrett clasped his hands. "Please . . . try."

Chris huffed and pulled his bear closer to his face. "Are we going to die?" He sounded better than before. A few of their classmates giggled.

"Very good, Chris." Ashley nodded at him. "You sound just like a baby."

"Thanks." Chris scowled.

Mr. Garrett covered his face with his hands. "Let's continue."

Landon as Hook walked toward the kids tied to the imaginary pole. "Now . . . you will walk the plank." He waved his hook so fast it came off and flew across the room. A group of nearby pirates had to duck so they wouldn't get hit.

Hook was defenseless! Also his pirates were shaken up. Suddenly Ashley had an idea. She shook her hands free of the rope and quick did the same for her pretend siblings. "Come on, boys!" she yelled. Then she ran to the front of the imaginary ship. "Grab your weapons. This is *our* ship now!"

No one moved. Everyone just stared at her.

"Ashley . . ." Natalie was fluttering around as Tinker Bell. She gave Ashley an anxious look. "What are you doing?"

"What I should have done a long time ago." Ashley walked over to the ship wheel prop and spun it a few times. She liked being captain.

Mr. Garrett waved the script in the air. "Ashley. You need to stay on book." Shock was all over his face. "Please . . . follow the script."

Only Ashley couldn't really hear him. She wasn't even in the classroom anymore. The wooden floor of the *Jolly Roger* creaked beneath her feet, and the salty Neverland sea sprayed her face.

Never mind walking the plank! Freedom was on the horizon for Wendy and her brothers.

And Ashley knew just where to take the ship.

"Tiger Lily, man the sails. Tinker Bell, you're on watch. Let's get outta here!"

Natalie seemed confused but committed. She used her hands as binoculars and surveyed the seas around them. Amy pretended to release the sails. And, with that, the girls were off.

Ashley stood on her tiptoes. "To Lake Monroe! For an adventure!" She pointed in the air, shouting loud enough for the room next door to hear.

Mr. Garrett sat back on the edge of his desk and shook his head. "This isn't the script."

"Wendy! You can't take my ship!" Landon was still trying to get his hook back on. He shuffled toward Ashley, like he was going to take the wheel from her.

"Wait!" Elliot stepped in front of Landon. "It's supposed to be *my* ship at the end of the scene!"

"Can't you see!" Landon whispered to Elliot. "I'm trying to get us back on track. . . ." He moved around Elliot and continued for Ashley. "Wendy Darling! You will regret this!" He took one more step and tripped over Chris's teddy bear. He fell with a loud *THWAP!*

Ashley gasped. "Hook? Are you okay?" She helped him up.

"I'm fine." Landon readjusted his hat. A goofy smile came over his face. Then he seemed to remember he was Captain Hook. He cleared his throat. "Wendy! I'll get you!"

"Stop!" Mr. Garrett stood on his chair this time. Everyone looked at him.

He rubbed his head and removed his glasses. "I think that's enough rehearsal for today."

Ashley marched over to her teacher. "Wait! It was just getting good! Why'd you stop us?"

"Because." Mr. Garrett looked tired. "That's not the *story*."

"I think it's better." She crossed her arms and tried to look like a superhero. "Wendy Darling takes over the ship! It's a hit, I tell you, Mr. Garrett."

"No." He managed a slight smile. "You're very . . . entertaining, Ashley. But that's not what J. M. Barrie wrote."

"Who?" Ashley wrinkled her nose.

"J. M. Barrie. The author who wrote the book." Mr. Garrett held up his copy of *Peter Pan*.

Ashley sucked in air through her teeth. "Ah. Yes. I thought he sounded familiar. Maybe he'd consider a rewrite." She shrugged. "Just a thought."

"You, miss, are the perfect Wendy. And you're a great leader." Mr. Garrett looked right at her. "But, Ashley, you need to stick with the lines. That's the only way a class play works."

"I just . . . I thought a trip to Lake Monroe would be fun." Ashley looked at her shoes. One of them was untied. It could wait till later.

"I know. But we have to be serious about this." He closed the script. "Try to act more grown-up, okay?" He turned to the class. "Please gather your things and study your lines tonight. Also tomorrow is . . ."

Everything faded.

Ashley couldn't stop her disappointment. Wasn't the whole point of *Peter Pan* to stay little? And now her teacher was telling her to grow up. Of all things.

She packed her bag, tied her shoe and helped put the props away. The last item to go back in the closet was the pirate ship wheel. She held it for a few seconds and then looked out the window. For one more moment, she was Wendy, taking the ship and maybe all the Lost Boys to Lake Monroe. Where they wouldn't have to worry about lines and parts and hooks flying across the room.

Where they didn't have to be grown-up, even for a few minutes. Instead they could be forever young.

At least for a little while longer.

13.

Dad's Career Day

KARI

The meteor shower was twelve days away and Kari couldn't wait. For now Ms. Nan's class was still working on their essays. What they wanted to be when they grew up. Every day they talked about a different career and today was the most exciting assignment of all.

Today was Take Your Child to Work Day! A day to go to work with their parents.

Kari had thought about it all night. A hospital might be the perfect place to work one day. She and Brooke and Ashley all had permission to join Dad from morning to night to see what a doctor actually did. Kari had her notebook so she could write down what she learned about working with sick people.

Kids like Alex.

They were driving to the hospital now, and Kari stared at the first page in her notebook. It read: Kari Baxter's Take Your Child to Work Day Observations. Observations were real things Kari might see or hear or experience today. Details she could use in her class essay.

Kari tapped her pencil. She felt like Lois Lane from the Superman comics. Or Nancy Drew, the famous fictional detective! Ashley and Brooke had to write reports on Career Day with their dad, too.

"Dad." Ashley sat next to Kari. Brooke was in the front passenger seat. "I want you to know something."

"Yes, Ashley." Dad smiled over his shoulder at her. "Tell me."

"I've thought about it." Ashley smoothed the wrinkles from her jeans. "And I feel ready to perform surgery today. If that's what we need to do."

Dad looked at Ashley in the rearview mirror. "No one will be performing surgery today."

"But I'm ready." Ashley held a finger up in the air. "I'm not afraid at all."

"Yes." Dad's voice was patient. "It takes more than courage to operate on someone, Ashley. You have to go to college many, many years for that."

Kari put her hand over her mouth so Ashley wouldn't hear her laugh. Her sister was hilarious.

Ashley was still trying to get into the operating room at Dad's hospital. "Here's something." She leaned forward. "What if someone *else* does the surgery? Can we just peek inside?"

"I think you're a little confused." Dad chuckled. "We will not be going near, nor will we be performing, *any* surgeries today." Dad paused. "Got it?"

Ashley's eyes got wide, and her mouth hung open. "I truly thought that was the whole point, Father. To take part in a surgery."

Kari tapped Ashley's shoulder.

"Yes?" Ashley turned to her. "Can I help you?"

"The point today is to learn more about different jobs and see what we enjoy." Kari looked at her notebook again. "Let's all collect observations. Then we can share them."

"I like that!" Brooke looked back at Kari and Ashley. "We can do that!"

Ashley smiled. "Maybe I could draw something."

"Exactly." Dad nodded. "There you go, Ashley."

Kari smiled at her dad in the mirror and took in a deep breath. In a few hours she would know if she wanted to be a doctor. They were entering the hospital for a behind-the-scenes look. Like Charlie Bucket heading into Willy Wonka's factory. She could hardly wait. In fact, the closer they got to Dad's work, the more Kari was sure a hospital was exactly where she wanted to work. And that there was nothing she'd rather be than a doctor.

Just like her dad.

An hour later Kari knew the truth.

Behind the scenes at the hospital was nothing like Willy Wonka's factory. The walls were a green shade of yellow, the lights hummed, and machines were always beeping. This was different from the part of the hospital where Alex stayed. There they had toys and bright colors in every room.

She flipped to an open page in her notebook:

Buzzing lights. No toys. Kind of . . . creepy.

Next Kari and her sisters sat in a stuffy room

156

watching a video on the life of a hospital employee. They were with a few other kids whose parents worked here. The place smelled like old coffee and cleaning supplies.

A friendly woman with beautiful dark skin and a hundred pretty braids stood nearby. She was in charge of the students for Career Day. Her name was Miss Brandy. She held a clipboard and tapped her foot to the upbeat music coming from the TV.

On the screen a professional-type woman said, "So you see"—her voice sounded smart—"there are several hospital jobs besides being a doctor or nurse." Pictures of workers came on the TV. The woman finished her point. "You could be a janitor, a receptionist, or you could work on the kitchen staff. You might work in X-ray or other diagnostic testing areas."

Kari thought about that. Die-agnostic? She pushed the idea from her mind. The idea that she might work at a hospital someday seemed less and less likely.

The video ended and Miss Brandy turned off the TV. "There you have it. An in-depth look at what we do around here. Any questions?"

Kari raised her hand. "Where's my dad?" She hoped maybe he could take them home early.

"Your father is with a patient. We'll go see him soon." Miss Brandy looked around. "Anyone else?"

"What sort of training do I need to be a janitor?" The question came from a boy who looked about Erin's age. He had spiky hair. "I love trash."

"Hmm." Miss Brandy paused. "I'm not quite sure about the training. But there's a role for everyone, especially at a hospital. Here, you can definitely find something that makes you happy."

The spiky-haired kid smiled. Satisfied.

Ashley raised her hand. "Miss Brandy?"

"Yes, Ashley?"

"Perhaps you could tell me where the surgery room is? I was hoping to watch an operation." She stood and nodded. "I believe that should be next."

Kari tugged on Ashley's sweater. "You better behave!" She clenched her teeth and spoke in a low tone.

"Don't!" Ashley frowned at her. Then she looked back at Miss Brandy. "Well?"

Miss Brandy's eyes looked like they might pop

out of her face. "I'm sorry. But you children will not be anywhere near an operating room."

"My sister is a comedian." Brooke patted Ashley's head. "She knows we can't perform surgery. We're just kids. But maybe one day."

Kari liked the sound of that. *We're just kids.* Sometimes it was hard to remember.

"That's good." Miss Brandy exhaled. Her face looked relieved. "Something to look forward to, Ashley. Growing up has its benefits."

Performing surgery? Kari didn't see that as a benefit.

Ashley took a seat and crossed her arms. She was clearly not pleased.

Brooke looked at Miss Brandy. "I was wondering about . . . what was it? Patient therapy?"

"Yes." Miss Brandy's face lit up. "Physical therapy."

"That's it." Brooke was beaming. She clearly loved this medical stuff.

For a few minutes, Miss Brandy told Brooke what physical therapy is. "It helps sick people get back to their everyday lives."

"That's cool." Brooke jotted something into her notebook.

Kari couldn't believe it. This medical stuff was like Christmas for Brooke.

Miss Brandy took everyone into the hall and to an empty hospital room where she explained various medical trinkets and tools. Kari tried to focus. With every hour she was more sure that working at a hospital wasn't her thing. Sure, her dad helped people. He even saved lives.

That didn't mean that she had to like it, too.

"Okay." Miss Brandy put her hand in the air. "Line up. We are going to go to the cafeteria, tour the kitchen, have some lunch, and then you can meet up with your parent or guardian."

The students followed Miss Brandy out of the room and down another hall. Kari was last in line, right behind Ashley. Suddenly commotion broke out behind them. Four people ran down the hallway pushing a stretcher and looking very nervous. They were shouting back and forth about something Kari couldn't understand.

It seemed scary and stressful.

That settled it. Kari never wanted to work in a hospital. Being a doctor was out of the question. She had no idea hospital work was so serious. Which meant there was something else she would one day have to do.

When she grew up.

But for the life of her, Kari couldn't figure out what that something was.

As Kari and her sisters ate lunch with the other kids on Career Day, Ashley kept the conversation lively.

"I'm Wendy." She shook Miss Brandy's hand. "Not sure you knew that."

Kari rolled her eyes and smiled. That Ashley.

"I didn't know." Miss Brandy studied the name tag on Ashley's sweater. "It says there, your name is Ashley."

"Yes, I know." Ashley peeled off the name tag and folded it into a tiny square. "That's my real name. It's confusing."

Miss Brandy definitely looked confused.

"Oh. . . . I'm Wendy in the Peter Pan play." Ashley did a single laugh as she looked around the table. "I should've started with that."

Pretty soon, though, Brooke cut into the conversation and the rest of lunch the talk was about doctors and specialties and operating. Kari was surprised they didn't break into a discussion about surgery again.

When she finished eating, Kari jotted six observations in her journal.

> Miss Brandy is nice. I wouldn't make a good janitor. Some people cook food at a hospital. Which is very needed, even if the food didn't taste the best. The walls are a strange color. I do NOT like the scary looks on the nurses' faces running down the hall.

She closed her notebook and looked at the nearby window. A bird fluttered onto a tree branch and the sun streamed through the scarce leaves. Kari sighed. She planted her elbows on the table and rested her chin in her hands.

I want to be outside with the birds, she thought. *Or dancing with my friends. Or learning history in Ms. Nan's class.* She took a bite of her salad. It tasted the same way the hospital smelled. Which gave Kari one more thought, the detail that probably best summed up her thoughts about working at the hospital. The observation was this:

I want to go home.

Kari realized that people needed to work at a hospital. They had to cook and clean and care for the patients. Patients like Alex. And all of them were gifted to do so. And they all seemed to like it. They had found what they were passionate about. And while Kari didn't really have a desire to follow a career path at a hospital, she was grateful for the people who did.

And in that moment, Kari knew her time at the hospital hadn't been a total disaster. In fact, she was glad she'd come along. Not because Career Day had shown her what she wanted to do when she grew up. But because it had done a very nice job of telling her what she did not want to do.

And that was at least part of the answer.

14

Career Day Confusion

ASHLEY

Ashley wasn't listening to the hospital conversation between Brooke and Miss Brandy. Because something amazing had happened! The nice woman had given them each a piece of paper with a list of jobs they could do at the hospital. And that was the highlight of lunch for one reason.

The page was the perfect kind for making a paper airplane.

So while everyone else at the table talked, Ashley folded the top right corner of the paper toward the center, then she did the same to the other side. A few more bends and tweaks and she had a fine-looking jet. Not just any jet.

This was a 747.

She held the plane up over her head and inspected it. "Whooosh," she whispered low. "You're going to fly across the whole cafeteria."

Before anyone could stop her, Ashley stood and held the plane high. Then with the exact right speed, she shot the paper jet through the air.

"Ashley!" Miss Brandy was on her feet now, too. "What are you doing?"

"Flying! Look at it!" Ashley didn't take her eyes off the plane. It drifted across the tables and chairs and came to an impressive landing just shy of a table of people in white coats. Doctors, probably.

"No." Miss Brandy's voice was louder than before. "That is unacceptable."

Before Ashley could run after her plane, Miss Brandy marched over and grabbed it from the floor. She was not holding it the most gentle way, which meant the wings were getting bent.

Miss Brandy returned to the table and set the damaged 747 down beside her. She raised her brow at Ashley. "We do not throw paper airplanes across the cafeteria!"

Kari and a few of the kids at the table smiled. But no one laughed.

Ashley waved her hand toward the rest of the room. "I think the people liked it. This place isn't very entertaining, Miss Brandy. If you haven't noticed."

At that, one girl let out a small giggle. But she slapped her hand over her mouth. Apparently no one wanted to take Ashley's side here.

"Ashley, sending paper airplanes across a room full of people can be dangerous." Miss Brandy pulled the paper jet closer to herself. "Please finish your lunch."

The dots were not connecting for Ashley. She raised her hand.

Miss Brandy let out a loud breath. "Yes, Ashley?"

"Excuse me . . . but how is it dangerous . . . watching a paper airplane soar overhead?"

For a few seconds Miss Brandy looked stumped. Then her face got more stern. "For one thing . . . you could poke someone's eye out!"

Ashley thought about that. "I will say . . . no better place to have your eye poked out than at a hospital." She looked around at the other kids. "Am I right?"

No one said a word.

"Right or wrong, the plane is mine now." Miss Brandy settled back into her seat and after a few seconds she picked up the conversation with Brooke and a couple other students.

Fine, Ashley thought. Her captured plane seemed to cry out to her from across the table where it sat. *Come get me . . . I want to fly.* "Not today, little jet," she whispered. "I'm so sorry. You have to stay in paper airplane jail."

Ashley leaned back and crossed her arms. Suddenly she felt bad about her paper airplane. And the way she'd talked to Miss Brandy. "Excuse me."

Miss Brandy raised her eyebrows. "Yes, Ashley?"

"I'm sorry." She really meant it. "You're right. Paper airplanes should be outside. Free. Like the birds."

"Yes." Miss Brandy smiled. "I agree. Thank you."

Ashley was glad that was behind her. Even still, she would have to tell Elliot that the hospital Career Day was a bust. They didn't get to perform surgery and they didn't see a single patient. She did, though, have a nice conversation with a cook named Lenny from Fort Lauderdale.

If she had to work at a hospital she would probably be the cook. Like Lenny.

After lunch they toured the emergency room, and Ashley and her sisters got to wait in their dad's office. He was almost finished for the day. When they were alone in the small room, Ashley saw the most beautiful sight.

Behind Dad's desk was a painting of an enormous boat sailing a stormy sea. It reminded Ashley of the pirate ship in *Peter Pan*! "Can you see me there?" She stood and walked to the painting.

Brooke and Kari stared at her. "In the painting?" Kari joined her near the piece of art. She squinted at the painted ship.

"Yes!" Ashley pointed to a window on the ship's lower half. "I'm in there." She held up her arms and let them fall to her sides. "Can't you see it? Wendy Darling." She tapped the canvas. "That's the ship Peter Pan took from Captain Hook, and I'm behind that window!"

Kari turned and stared at her. For a long time. Finally she shook her head. "You're one in a million, Ashley. That's for sure."

Just then the door swung open and Dad stepped inside. "Hey, girls!" He smiled. "Here I am!" He sat at his desk. He wore a white coat like the people in the cafeteria. "How was the day?"

Brooke was beaming. Even her cheeks were all lit up. "I know for sure I want to be a doctor, Dad." She ran to him and hugged his neck. "This was the best day all year!"

Kari came next. She admitted that working at a hospital wasn't for her. "It doesn't smell good."

Dad laughed. "You get used to it. But I understand, Kari. Being a doctor isn't for everyone."

"It's not for me, either." Ashley put her hand on her father's shoulder. "But I did meet a nice cook named Lenny from Fort Lauderdale."

Dad, Kari and Brooke all looked at her. Like they were trying to figure her out.

Finally their dad chuckled. "Maybe you'll be a cook, Ashley."

"No." She pointed to the artwork behind the desk. "I'm going to make paintings like this one."

Everyone agreed and Dad hugged her close. "You'll be the best artist in all the world!"

His words stayed with Ashley the rest of the day and even as her family sat down to dinner that night. "Dad says it's okay if I don't work at a hospital." Ashley grinned at him. "Because I'll be the best artist in the world."

Their mother nodded. "He's right, Ash. If you work hard and keep drawing, there really are no limits!"

Ashley liked that. No limits. It was the way she'd felt about her paper airplane until Miss Brandy took it. "One question." Ashley turned to Dad. "That whole ivy thing. Why do the patients need ivy?" She looked around at Mom and her siblings. "Ivy makes me itch."

A happy laugh came from their father. "Honey, we give them an IV. It's a tube we put in the veins of many patients. That tube helps us give them medicine."

"Wow! I had no idea." Ashley gave him a

thumbs-up. "I will say, Dad, that's very impressive. Whoever thought of it."

Next, Luke talked about helping Mom at the shelter downtown. But the whole time Ashley studied her dad. He looked happy. Even though he'd been dealing all day with bloody cuts and broken bones, beeping noises and very sick patients. He barely had time to visit with Ashley and her sisters, or eat lunch today. Still he came home happy.

Every day Dad helped Mom in the kitchen and he helped Ashley and the rest with their homework. If his work made him tired or sad, he never brought that home.

He knew how to carry the heavy.

Which was a gift. Like a superpower.

Kari took a bite of her meat loaf. "Well, all I know is the best part was when we left the hospital and went outside." She jabbed her fork in their father's direction. "We played tag with Dad."

"Hey, that almost rhymes!" Luke hit the table a few times. "We played tag, uh-uh-uh . . . with our Dad, uh-uh-uh!"

Ashley joined in, pounding the table till the glasses rattled. Kari stood and danced around the table with Erin, and Brooke dinged her glass with the fork. "We played tag, uh-uh-uh . . . with our Dad, uh-uh-uh!"

Mom and Dad watched in sheer delight. At least it seemed that way. And when the moment was over, the kids took their seats again. Ashley slid her chair close to the table. "You're welcome." She smiled and nodded. "For that performance."

"Yes, thank you! Wow!" Mom laughed and looked at Dad. "I mean, John. We could have our own show."

"At Dollywood, maybe! Or Branson, Missouri." Dad gestured like he was reading off a billboard. "The Five Baxters perform their wondrous talents for the world!"

"I like it." Brooke giggled. "It would be fun!" She was out of breath from the dancing and drumming.

The family kept singing through dishes and homework. Kari practiced her "Under the Sea" dance and Ashley ran through her Wendy lines with Luke.

Before bed, Ashley walked to her parents' room to say good night and she overheard Brooke talking to Mom about going to medical school. Ashley listened long enough to be nervous.

Was Brooke going to move out for college? Even before high school? Why was she in such a hurry to grow up? Peter Pan would be disappointed. Which gave Ashley an idea.

Maybe she should make a pledge for all the Baxter kids. They could agree that no matter what . . . there would be no college or medical school or finding a career. They would live here forever, doing dinnertime dances and hanging out at their rock and taking adventures in their backyard. Each of them could help write the paper and they would all sign it. After that the matter would be settled.

The Baxter kids would never grow up!

15

The Mystery of the Missing Bracelet

KARI

The talent show was in less than a week and Kari's mind was jam-packed. She had a swim meet Wednesday. Another practice for the talent show was tonight with Mandy and Liza. She hadn't started the essay on her future career. And she still didn't know what that career might possibly be.

It was Saturday afternoon and Kari sat with her notebook and pen in the backyard on a blanket next to Bo. Kari ran her fingers through his soft, furry coat until Bo stood, yawned and circled a few times. Then he curled into a ball beside Kari and fell asleep.

"Oh, Bo." Kari rubbed his ears. "You have no worries at all."

She looked down at her notebook. All she had written was

When I grow up, I want to be . . .

That was it.

She thought about the zoo employees, and the farmer who visited her class. Also a senator who had talked to them, and then the visit to the hospital. But she didn't love any of those jobs. She was beginning to worry that she'd never get this essay finished.

She jotted something on the paper that she knew the answer to:

8 Days until the meteor shower!

A bird squawked in the distance and Bo lifted his head. He sniffed the air and took off barking. At the same instant, Ashley came outside with a plate of sliced apples.

"Hey." She set the plate down and took a seat next to Kari. "I think it's time."

"For what?" Kari took an apple slice.

"You know." Ashley leaned back on her hands. "For a sister heart-to-heart talk."

Kari laughed. "A heart-to-heart?"

"Yes." Ashley bit into her apple. "You tell me what's on your heart, and I tell you what's on mine."

"Okay . . ." Kari closed her notebook.

"I'll go first!" Ashley stared straight at Kari. "I think we need to write a pledge and sign it. All us Baxter kids."

"A pledge?" Kari had no idea where this was going. "What kind of pledge?"

"Like a contract . . . a promise." Ashley chewed her apple and swallowed before finishing her thought. "A pledge to stay young forever. A never-grow-up contract!"

Kari laid down on her side, too. "You mean, make a promise to never get older?" She squinted. "Doesn't everyone grow up?"

"Usually." Ashley sat up, more serious. "But if

we all agree to stay young forever. To not think about medical school or careers or even middle school . . ."

"Or what we want to be when we grow up!" Kari jumped to her feet. "I think you're onto something here."

"Exactly!" Ashley sat up, too. She clapped a few times. "Now you're getting it."

For a while they were quiet. Just the breeze in the orange and yellow trees and the sound of the birds overhead. Kari sighed. "I do wish we could stay this way forever." She studied the sky. It was bright blue today. Peaceful. "I'm stuck on this assignment for school. We have to write an essay about what we want to be when we grow up."

"Already?" Ashley sounded shocked. The way she'd sounded when she found out the kids wouldn't be operating on anyone during Career Day.

Kari nodded. "It's just . . . I don't know what I want to do when I'm older."

Ashley paused. "I heard Brooke telling Mom that she wants to go to medical school. Which is what got me thinking . . ."

"About the pledge?" Kari turned to her sister.

"Yes. If Luke, and Brooke, and Erin agree with us to stay young forever, then we'd have to do it. We'd find a way. Somehow." Ashley's excitement faded as she talked. "Right?"

"It's worth a try." Kari fumbled with the pencil in her hand. "I'll sign it. I think everyone else will, too. Except maybe Brooke."

"Okay." Ashley sounded determined again. "I'll write the pledge today."

Kari smiled. "Good." The pledge was a nice idea. Perfect, actually. But how would it work?

"Kari . . . Ashley?" Mom called from the back porch. "Come here, please." The girls hurried to her.

Mom's face looked worried. "Girls. I've lost my bracelet. The one your father gave me on our wedding day." She rubbed her hands together. "Have you seen it?"

Ashley held her hands up. "I didn't take it!" She shook her head. "After almost going to zoo jail, I swore off a life of crime."

A smile tugged at their mom's mouth. Ashley could make anyone happy. Even in the middle of a crisis. "I'm not accusing you, honey." Mom took gentle hold of Ashley's cheeks. "Just asking."

"Hmm." Kari began to pace. "Where was the last place you had it?"

Mom thought about this. "In the kitchen, I think . . ."

"Let's go!" Kari took her mom's hand and led her and Ashley into the kitchen. Kari had learned to write down observations at Take Your Child to Work Day. She had a good feeling about this. "If anyone can solve your case, Mother, it'll be me." She tapped the counter near the sink. "Was it here?"

"Exactly." Mom nodded. "I had it on . . . I was doing dishes. And . . ." She walked over to the sink. "I took it off to wash my hands!"

Kari turned to the next blank page in her journal. She wrote the first clue:

Took off bracelet to wash hands.

"Got it." Kari put the pencil behind her ear. She walked a few feet one direction, then the other.

179

"Kari." Ashley studied her. "What are you doing?"

"We need to solve the case. The case of the missing bracelet!" Kari crouched superlow, so she could examine the baseboards. "It's not here."

Mom sat at the table. "I hope it's not lost. I'll go check the van and my room again. Just in case." She hurried out of the kitchen.

"It has to be *somewhere*. Right?" Ashley joined Kari on the floor.

"Right. That's the perfect truth to begin with." Kari stood up again. "The fact that her bracelet has to be somewhere."

Brooke came into the kitchen and grabbed a glass of water. She had just finished a bike ride around their yard. "What are you two doing?"

"Mom lost her bracelet." Kari looked at Ashley. An idea hit her. "The Baxter Kids Detective Agency is on the case." She smiled at Brooke. "You can join if you want."

Brooke seemed slightly amused, but she shrugged. "Can't. I need to do homework." She took one last drink of her water and set the cup in the sink.

"Aha!" Kari returned to the sink. "What if it fell down the sink?" She put her hand down the kitchen drain, feeling around for anything that resembled the bracelet.

Nothing.

Brooke started to leave.

"Wait!" Ashley called out. "Come on, Brooke. Help us. We're having fun."

"I don't have time for kid games." Brooke frowned. "I have real work to do."

Erin came into the kitchen and sat on the counter. "I'll help."

"See?" Brooke pointed to their youngest sister as she left the kitchen. "You have Erin. That's plenty of detectives. You don't need me."

Kari and Ashley and Erin watched her go.

Ashley shrugged. "Fine. Brooke's right. Who needs her anyway?" She turned to Kari. "Where to next?"

"I've been thinking." All of a sudden Kari pointed to the cupboard under the sink. "The trash! Let's check there."

"Why?" Erin peered around Kari.

"Because . . ." Kari opened the cabinets. "Maybe Mom's bracelet accidentally slid off the counter and into the trash bin." Kari pulled the trash can out and set it on the floor. The thing was full to the brim. "Yikes." Kari plunged her hand into the garbage and sorted through banana peels and empty cans of dog food and apple peelings.

The smell was ripe.

"Ew!" Erin held her nose. She backed up a few feet.

"I'll help!" Ashley dug her hands in, too. "Let's find it!"

"What're you doing?" Luke bounced the basketball into the kitchen. Kari could feel him standing behind her. "Why are you digging in the trash?"

Erin was still holding her. "They're looking for Mom's bracelet. It's lost."

"Awesome!" He dropped to his knees and pushed up his sleeves.

"Thanks, Luke!" Kari smiled at him. Luke was the best little brother. "You are now officially part of the Baxter Kids Detective Agency. This is our first case."

"Great!" He began to sift through the trash. "Which bracelet did she lose?"

Ashley pulled a bag of moldy grapes from the garbage. "Her gold one." She peered into the slimy bag. "Not here." She dropped the grapes back into the can.

When they reached the bottom, Luke stood and held up his hands. They were covered in slime. "That's the last of the trash." He washed his hands in the sink. "Where next, fellow detectives?"

Kari and Ashley washed their hands, too. Who knew trash could smell so bad? Kari jotted down this detail in her notebook:

Not in the trash.

She tapped her pencil to the paper. "I was sure it would be there."

Then a thought hit Kari. She walked to the back door. If it wasn't on the kitchen counter or in the sink . . . and if it wasn't in the trash can . . . then where was it?

Erin joined her. "Maybe we should look outside?"

"Why would it be out there?" Ashley came to the door and Luke followed her.

Kari nodded. "I like it. Maybe it slipped off while she was in the garden."

"Let's go!" Luke led the parade outside to the garden. They checked between the zucchini and squash and carrots. Then they searched the bushes and the flower beds, and around the trees.

The four of them marched out to the front porch and then to the mailbox, and up the driveway.

Kari prayed as they searched. *It's a small thing, God. But it matters to Mom. Please help us find it.*

They came full circle to the back porch again. Kari and her siblings sat on the steps like deflated balloons. Hopeless.

"I really thought we were going to find it." Kari dug her elbows into her knees and slouched. Being a detective made her tired.

Luke stood and stared at the vast backyard. His baseball cap kept the sun from his eyes. "It has to be somewhere."

"That's our motto." Kari stood next to Luke. "It hasn't helped much."

Suddenly Ashley pointed. "What about Bo?"

"Hmm." Kari hadn't thought about that yet. Bo loved shiny things, and he chewed on everything. "It's possible."

"No." Luke called Bo over. Their dog looked innocent. Luke patted his head. "Bo wouldn't steal Mom's bracelet."

"Maybe as an accident." Ashley jumped around. "It's possible."

"Ashley's right." Brooke's voice came from behind them. "We should check Bo's bed."

Kari spun around. Their older sister stood in the doorway. Kari held out her arms. "Brooke!"

Ashley stood and hugged Brooke. "You made it!"

"If there's still a spot for me . . . I'm in." She looked a little embarrassed. But whatever had happened before this didn't matter. Brooke was here now.

"Of course there's a spot." Luke shook Brooke's hand. "Welcome to the Baxter Kids Detective Agency. This is our first case."

Brooke laughed. "I have a lot to do . . . but I never want to be too busy for you four."

"Well, come on, people!" Kari clapped her hands. "We have a bracelet to find." Kari marched them inside to Bo's fluffy bed. And there, tucked deep in the fabric, was Mom's beautiful gold bracelet. Covered in slobber and dirt. But it was there!

Kari held it up. "We found it! We found it!" Kari and her siblings shouted as they rushed into Mom and Dad's room with her bracelet.

"I can't believe it." Happy tears filled Mom's eyes. "I've been praying!"

"Me, too." Kari handed the dirty bracelet to Mom. Kari shrugged. "I guess God's the leader of our detective agency."

"Good call." Mom dabbed at her eyes. "He knows everything."

Dad smiled. "I'd say your first case was a huge success!"

Mom took the bracelet to her bathroom and washed it. Then she put it where it belonged. Back on her wrist.

A few minutes later Kari found a spot next to Bo on the sofa. She still needed to work on her essay. But their detective work had been a great change of pace. Kari's head didn't feel so full now.

"Okay, Bo." Kari ran her hand over his soft head. "Did you do that on purpose?"

Bo didn't say anything, of course. But Kari was almost certain she saw something on their dog's cute face.

A happy smile.

16

Balance Beam of Life

ASHLEY

Ashley started the game by drawing a man.
Mr. Garrett was talking about math
shortcuts at the front of the room, but
the game was way more fascinating. Ashley passed
the picture to Elliot. The plan was for Elliot to add
something to it. He would then pass it to Natalie,
who would add something. And the drawing would
come back to Ashley.

Natalie hadn't been sure. "I don't want to get in
trouble," she whispered.

"We only get in trouble if we get caught." Elliot
had rubbed his hands together. "This will be inter-
galactic!"

If aliens ever invaded Earth, Ashley would want

to be on Elliot's team. She was sure about that.

Now they were on the game's sixth round, and the man in the picture was getting funnier each time. He currently had wings, and roller skates, and he wore a helmet. He held a bouquet of balloons and a parrot sat perched on his shoulder.

"There's a trick to learning your nines," Mr. Garrett was saying, "when it comes to multiplication. What you want to do is . . ."

Ashley tuned him out. She took the picture from Natalie and stared at it. Natalie's last turn had added a mustache and glasses to the man. Without meaning to, Ashley let out a sudden laugh.

It sounded loud, even to her.

In a flash, Mr. Garrett was directly in front of her desk. His mouth bunched up, like he was eating a lemon. "What is that?" He pointed to the drawing.

Ashley smiled. "Hi . . ." She did a slight wave at their teacher. "This . . ." She folded the drawing and held it close. "Was just a great way to pass the time."

"Pass the *time*?" Mr. Garrett's eyebrows raised, higher than she had seen a man's eyebrows go. "This is math, Ashley. Not free time."

"It was my idea." Elliot stood. "I'm the problem here."

"Actually, I believe I'm the problem." Ashley nodded. "Because that seems to be a pattern."

Natalie threw her hands up. "And I tried to stop them."

Mr. Garrett reached out. "Let me see it."

190

Ashley pressed the drawing to her stomach. "I'm a bit reluctant to give it up, if I'm honest . . ." It was kind of a masterpiece. What if Mr. Garrett threw it out? She cleared her throat. "Perhaps I could have a few minutes to decide."

"No, Ashley." Her teacher kept his hand extended. "Give it to me. Now!"

About that time, Ashley noticed the rest of the class. They were all staring at her. Natalie was shaking her head very fast. Like a warning system.

Ashley sank a bit. "Fine. I'm sorry for causing a disturbance. Really." She handed over the drawing. "I would like to state, though, that the drawing is mine. So please . . . sir, can I at least get it back? Later, maybe? When it's convenient? Or perhaps as an early Christmas—"

"Stop talking, Ashley." Mr. Garrett studied the drawing and Ashley was sure she saw him smile. He folded it up and closed his eyes. He exhaled.

"Pretty funny." Ashley whispered. Hopeful. "Yes?"

Mr. Garrett removed his glasses. "Ashley, you and Elliot and Natalie will stay inside today during recess and clean the chalkboards." He was still holding the drawing. "Math is not a chance to pass the time."

"But . . ." Ashley remembered something. "I don't want to be a criminal. I promised myself. And my parents."

"You are not a criminal." Mr. Garrett looked at her. "But there are consequences."

"Ha!" Chris called out from the back. "That's what you get for passing notes!"

Ashley turned around. Landon covered his face with his hand. Possibly this moment might make him think twice about being friends with Chris.

Mr. Garrett pointed at Chris. "You will join them."

"What?" Chris threw his hands in the air. "What did I do?"

Mr. Garrett made a sharp turn back to the front of the room. He set the drawing on his desk. "That's all, Chris. We will now get back to math shortcuts."

Landon raised his hand.

"Yes?" Mr. Garrett looked ready to call it a day.

For a few seconds, Landon seemed to collect

his thoughts. "Mr. Garrett, Ashley was just having fun." He tried to smile, but it didn't quite work out. "Could they have a second chance?"

"Mr. Blake . . . do you want to join them?"

"No! I was just saying . . . it doesn't seem like they did any harm." Landon stopped there.

"Landon, Chris, Ashley, Elliot and Natalie . . ." Mr. Garrett had officially run out of patience. "You will *all* clean the boards during recess. He turned to the chalkboard. "Where were we?"

Ashley gave Landon a quick look. "Thanks." She whispered the word very soft.

He smiled and nodded.

Ashley turned her attention to the front of the classroom. How about that! Landon Blake had stuck up for her. He wasn't only her friend, apparently.

He was on her side.

And that made Ashley smile all the way through math.

Cleaning the boards turned out to be a hoot. Ashley and Natalie and the boys raced to see who was the fastest cleaner. And then they tried synchronized cleaning. Ashley laughed harder than she had all day at that fun.

Before school ended she and the chalkboard gang told Mr. Garrett they were sorry. They were. Because passing time during math was the wrong thing to do.

Ashley told her mom and dad about the criminal act later that evening, when everyone else was in bed.

"I'm sorry, Father . . . Mother." Ashley hung her head. "It was very childish." She looked up. "Which is actually my goal lately. Being young. Not growing up." She smiled. Then she remembered the point here. "Anyway, I am sorry."

Dad looked straight at her. "I'm glad you're sorry." He hugged her. "And please, Ashley, keep your drawings in your sketchbook from now on."

Which was what she did that night. A perfect drawing of a man with wings, and roller skates and a helmet. He held a bouquet of balloons and a parrot sat perched on his shoulder. And he had a mustache and glasses.

She was still thinking about that silly picture the next day at gymnastics, as she stood in line for the balance beam.

"Ashley. You're up!" Coach Beth called out.

"Oh . . . sorry." She stepped forward and took a deep breath. The balance beam stretched out in front of her. It was the only thing in gymnastics she hadn't quite conquered. She could do a cartwheel, and somersaults, and the bear crawl and the splits. But every time she stepped up to the balance beam, she got nervous. Or she got more excited about the foam pit.

But not today.

Ashley knew that she needed to get across. That she *would* get across. She stepped onto the beam and felt her ankles wiggle. She closed her eyes and exhaled. She took one step, and then another.

"Good girl, Ash. Keep going," Coach Beth yelled from the other side.

Suddenly the balance beam felt like life itself. With every step, she could feel herself getting older. *Just grow up*, people kept saying. *Act your age.* Ashley took another step and she could see herself finishing elementary school. Step. Step. She was figuring out middle school and then navigating high school.

Another step.

Here she was, growing up too fast. She needed to find a way to Neverland. *Help,* she called out inside herself. *I don't want to grow up this fast. Someone stop the clock!*

She stopped midbeam. She looked one way, then the other. A wobble started, but this time she caught herself. She wasn't getting older with every step. That wasn't true. She was a fifth-grade girl trying to cross the balance beam without falling.

An idea came to her! Suddenly the pit wasn't foam pieces. It was choppy, windy ocean water! And the balance beam was Captain Hook's plank! Of course it was, because she was Wendy! And maybe if she made it all the way across she would be in Neverland!

Maybe this was the way there!

You can do this, she told herself. She had walked the plank every day in Mr. Garrett's class during play rehearsal. This was no different. Ashley bent her knees and took another step. And another. One step at a time . . . until . . .

She jumped off the beam to the floor on the other side and raised both hands. She had done it! She had crossed the balance beam without falling.

"Hooray! You did it!" Marsha, her neighbor friend, greeted Ashley on the other side. She clapped and cheered along with the others on Ashley's team.

Ashley had conquered the balance beam and it was the best feeling ever. She jumped around with Marsha and walked it three more times before gymnastics was over. And no one ever knew that every time she crossed it, she wasn't walking the balance beam at all. No. She was walking Captain Hook's plank.

There was only one problem.

She still hadn't found a way to Neverland.

17

Under the Sea

KARI

Ms. Nan's entire class was buzzing for one reason.

Today the outlines for their essays were due. Kari couldn't believe how happy her classmates were. Even Mandy and Liza. Apparently everyone knew what they wanted to be when they grew up.

Everyone but her.

Kari listened to Ms. Nan once more explain the format of an outline: introduction, three supporting points, and a closing. "We've been talking about this for more than a month." She glanced around the class. "I'm sure most of you have your outline completed by now. In case you don't, I'll give you the next hour to get something on paper."

Ms. Nan had to approve their outlines before they could move on to writing. Kari sat back hard in her seat. The blankest piece of paper in all the world sat on her desk. She used the first ten minutes to write in her journal instead.

Dear God,

I need a lot of help down here. I have no idea what I want to do when I grow up, but the outline is due today! In 55 minutes! I knew that, of course. And still . . . nothing! This assignment has been stress in my head ever since Ms. Nan brought it up. What I'm saying is, please, could You help me?

Thanks!

Love, KB

P.S. Four days till the meteor shower!

They were allowed to walk around and chat with their neighbors during the outline time. "Sharing ideas creates more ideas," Ms. Nan always said.

Just then Kari felt a tap on her shoulder.

"Hey." Liza leaned over. "Your paper is empty." She grinned. "Being nothing might sound fun, but I don't think it's an option."

"Thanks, Liza." Kari tapped her pencil on her desk. "I actually think you might be onto something." She laughed and some of her stress melted away. "Being nothing could probably be my answer. I'd be good at it, I believe."

"You could try." Liza giggled. Then she looked at Kari's blank page again. "You really can't think of *anything*?"

Kari shook her head. "Nope." She blew a piece of hair out of her face. "Going to my dad's work didn't even help."

"Yeah." Liza sighed. "Me either. My mom is a banker . . . *boring*!" She gave a thumbs-down.

"So what did you put?" Kari rested her cheek on the desk.

"Law school." Liza looked proud of herself. "My dad says I'm smart enough." She stood and paced the aisle between their desks. "I can already see myself giving closing arguments."

"Arguments?" Kari didn't understand. "You're going to argue for a living?"

Liza laughed. "Something like that."

That didn't sound fun at all. Kari's shoulders slumped.

"Oh, Kari." Liza shrugged. "It's okay. You're good at lots of things."

Mandy skipped over. "What are we talking about?"

"Our friend here doesn't know what she wants to do when she grows up." Liza stood at Kari's side and patted her head.

"I'm definitely considering being nothing." Kari didn't break a smile this time.

"It's okay not to know, Kari." Mandy nodded. "That's why we try new things."

"But I have to know now." Time was running out. Kari could feel tears in her eyes. "What about you, Mandy?"

"I'm going to be an Olympic swimmer!" Mandy pretended to be at the end of a diving board, her knees bent, hands stretched out. She dropped the pose. "That's basically what I'm training for now on the swim team."

Liza grinned at Mandy. "I'll be there when you win your medal." She patted Kari's back. "Let's say we all go!"

"Okay." Kari sighed. "Time shouldn't be a problem. Since I won't be working."

"Perfect." Liza clapped a few times. She grabbed Mandy's hand and held it up. "You'll win the gold medal, Mandy! I can see it now. The swim team reunited at the Olympics."

This isn't helping, Kari thought. "I'm going to talk to Ms. Nan . . ." Kari stood and walked to her teacher's desk. She held out her blank piece of paper. "I'm having a problem." She didn't want to cry, but she was close.

Ms. Nan leaned closer to Kari. "What is it?"

Kari pointed to the empty page. "I don't know what I want to do . . . when I grow up." She sniffed. "I might . . . need a little more time."

"Of course, Kari." Ms. Nan came around the desk. She put her hand on Kari's shoulder. "This assignment isn't meant to overwhelm you. It's supposed to be fun!" Ms. Nan kneeled down so she could look at Kari's eyes. "This essay isn't going to decide your future. You may pick something and change your mind. And that's okay."

Kari nodded.

Ms. Nan handed Kari back her empty paper. "Why don't you get me an outline by Monday." She smiled. "How does that sound?"

"Really?" Kari looked straight at her teacher. "Ms. Nan, that would be the greatest gift."

"Remember . . . it's supposed to be *fun*!" Ms. Nan winked. "You can do this."

"Thank you, Ms. Nan." Kari took a deep breath and felt the weight leave her shoulders. She was very thankful for this chat with her teacher. And even more thankful for her teacher's kindness. Kari made her way back to her desk.

"Feel better?" Mandy gave Kari an understanding smile.

Kari nodded. "Much."

"Good!" Liza looked relieved. "Last swim meet of the season tonight. We need to be in fine form."

"Oh, don't worry!" Mandy took her pose again. "I'm always in fine form."

The swim meet! Kari had forgotten all about it. She had to work on her outline. Plus, she had hoped the three of them could stay after school to practice their "Under the Sea" dance.

Instead she was actually going to be under the sea—in the city swimming pool.

By the time Kari and her family walked into the rec center's indoor pool, Kari felt sick. The last thing she wanted was to swim tonight.

Sure, swimming had been fun at first. Kari had met Mandy and Liza that way. But now she was just sticking out the season because she didn't want to disappoint her friends. Deep down Kari didn't like swimming indoors. She didn't care for the chlorine smell in her hair; and she hated feeling cold after she got out of the pool.

She wondered if Mandy knew how many hours she would need to spend in this place to make it to the Olympics.

Kari's family found a spot in the bleachers and

she walked toward her team. "I'm nervous." She set her bag down next to Liza's and Mandy's.

"Why?" Liza stretched one arm, then the other. "We'll be fine."

Kari shook out her legs to loosen them up. "I'm distracted. The outline. The essay. The talent show. The meteor shower."

"You can't do any of those things right now." Mandy took a sip of water and adjusted her swim cap. "My mom always says, 'Do the next thing because that's all you can do.'"

Do the next thing. Kari ran those words through her mind a few times. "I like that, Mandy. Do the next thing." She looked at the pool a few feet away. "Right now the next thing is the swim meet!"

"Exactly." Mandy grinned. "Everything else will still be there later."

"Wow!" Liza nodded. "I'm going to use that one next time we have a math test. I missed a problem on the last one." She put her hands on her hips. "I never miss a problem."

The girls jumped in the pool and Kari put her goggles on. "Do the next thing," she whispered.

Then she began swimming her warm-up laps. Because that was next.

During the relay, Kari's brain focused better than it had all day. Because there was room in her head now, that's why. Her whole attention was on swimming. This new way of thinking was a gift, the one she had asked God for! At one point she even imagined she was a mermaid blazing through the water.

Not till she finished her leg of the race and she was out of the pool did she hear how loud everyone was cheering. Especially her family.

"Kari, you're the best!" Ashley was jumping up and down, waving her hands. "Everyone! That's my sister right there!"

"She's my sister, too!" Luke also jumped around.

Kari waved at them. She really did have the best family ever.

Just then Coach Miller ran up. "Kari! That was your fastest time of the season!" She high-fived Kari. "Come on, let's cheer for Liza!"

Liza blazed through the water like usual. But this time she seemed a little faster, too. Cheryl swam the third leg. Cheryl was in a different class in school, but she was nice. This might not have been her day, because their relay team slipped to third place after Cheryl's swim.

Ashley and Liza and Coach Miller surrounded her as she climbed out of the pool. "Good job!" Kari clapped. "You did your best!"

Mandy was next. She had to move them from third place to first if they were going to win.

"You can do it, Mandy!" Coach Miller cupped her hands around her mouth, her shout filled the building.

"Go, Mandy!" Kari and Liza and Cheryl all yelled at the same time. "Faster!"

Bit by bit, Mandy actually did it. She moved into second place and then just before she touched the wall she swam into the lead.

"Wow!" Liza sounded surprised. "She really *could* do the Olympics."

Mandy got out of the water and joined Kari and the others. "We did it! We won!"

Kari wanted to remind Mandy that she, alone, had taken them from third to first place. But then . . .

that wasn't true. The relay was a team effort.

Just like friendship, Kari thought. *When one person is down, the others pick her up.*

She thought again about Mandy's advice. *Do the next thing.* Then Kari remembered Ms. Nan giving her extra time for her outline, and Mandy and Liza cheering her up at school earlier.

"Great work." Coach Miller pulled the relay swimmers into a huddle. "Win or lose . . . I'm proud of you. But today was a win. The best of the season." She put her hand in the middle of the circle. "Great season! Hands in. Teamwork on three . . . one, two, three!"

"Teamwork!" Kari and her teammates shouted.

Again Kari looked up in the stands at her family. They were still clapping and cheering. Showing their support. Kari could only hope her parents would be as supportive if she failed Ms. Nan's essay. *Don't think about that,* she told herself. *Not yet.*

That night when it was time for bed, Kari tiptoed to her parents' room. She knocked on the door.

"Come in." Dad called out.

Kari opened the door. Her parents sat up in bed reading. She made her way to them.

"There's our swimming star!" Mom looked proud of her.

"It was my fastest time. Because I decided to do the next thing." Kari looked from her mom to her dad. "That came from Mandy."

"I like that. 'Do the next thing' keeps you focused on the only thing you can actually do." Dad set his book down. "That was nice of Mandy, to share that with you."

Mom nodded. "Friends are important. On a team . . . and in life."

"Exactly." Kari sat on the edge of the bed. "My head has been too full to even smile lately."

Mom ran her hands over Kari's hair. "You haven't figured out your essay yet?"

Kari shook her head. "How am I supposed to know what I want to do when I'm older? It's hard enough being in sixth grade."

Dad chuckled. "You know . . . you're right, Kari." His laughter died down. "Still . . . I think Ms. Nan only wants you to pick something. Anything. It gives you a chance to learn a little more about something you could possibly do when you're older."

The way Dad put it, picking a topic didn't sound all that bad. "So I could pick anything, really?"

"Yes." Her mother patted her hand. "It's just meant to get you thinking."

"Okay." Kari crossed her arms. That revelation changed everything. She sighed. "Also, I don't know if we're ready for the talent show."

"I can help with that." Mom raised her hand. "Let's get the costumes and props tomorrow after school." Mom took Kari's hand and gave it a gentle squeeze. "Everything is going to be fine."

Dad's expression looked kind. "Responsibilities are part of growing up. Sounds like you're experiencing a little of that. More things to do . . . and less time to do them in."

"But . . ." Mom leaned in close to Kari. "Another part of growing up is knowing when to ask for help. It takes a mature girl to do that."

"Sometimes I just don't know what I need help with." Kari didn't want to pretend everything was perfect. "I get so . . . so anxious." She smiled at

Dad. "I wrote a prayer in my journal today. Just like you said."

"Did it help?" Dad's voice was the nicest of any father anywhere.

Kari grinned. "It did help! Mandy gave me that little pre–swim meet wisdom about doing the next thing. And I swam my fastest time ever. So, yes!"

"Good." Dad sighed. "Life isn't always easy. But we have each other."

"You're going to be wonderful, Kari." Mom assured her. "Essay or not, who you are going to be when you grow up is successful, and brave, and a hard worker. You'll be a good friend and someone who prays for help. Whatever field you do that in . . . it really doesn't matter. What matters is the kind of girl you are." Mom put her hand alongside Kari's cheek. "And you, Kari Baxter, are growing up to be a pretty extraordinary one."

Kari loved that her parents knew what to say. They always helped. Why hadn't she talked to them earlier? Her family didn't just cheer for her at a swim meet. They cheered for her always, through the good days and the harder ones.

Even now.

"Thank you, Mom . . . Dad." Kari hugged them both. "I needed this."

"Anytime." Dad kissed her cheek. "It's all going to work out. Don't forget Mandy's advice. Do the next thing."

"Yes." Kari felt peace and excitement as she walked to her bedroom and slipped into bed. Whatever career she chose, she most wanted to be in a family like this one. Where people cared and cheered and took time for hugs. Kari yawned and settled into her pillow. It was time to do the next thing.

And like that, she drifted off to sleep.

18

A New Neverland

ASHLEY

The Friday night talent show was in two hours and Ashley could hardly breathe.

She stood in the bathroom next to Kari, while Mom curled her hair. What was left of it, anyway, after Elliot and the gum disaster a month ago.

"It's grown out some." Mom smiled at her in the mirror.

Kari nodded. "She's right. It looks longer, Ash. For sure."

Ashley studied herself. "You know what? I think it *is* longer." She grinned. "Which is ideal, because Wendy has never had a gum disaster." She gave her dress a gentle tug. "Thank you for making this dress, Mother. I actually *am* Wendy in this thing."

They had bought the pale blue dress at the store, but there had been no sash or ruffles or lace. So Mom added all those things. Ashley shot Kari a look. "You absolutely look like a mermaid. In case you wondered."

"Thank you." Kari plugged her nose. She twisted to the floor and back up again. Liza's mom had added sequins to all the Dancing Queens' shirts and they each wore black jeans. "I feel like a mermaid."

Ashley turned her head so Mom could do another curl. "The sparkly sequins are altogether effervescent." She gave Mom a thumbs-up. "P.S. . . . I still like that word."

Mom laughed. "Almost as effervescent as you, Ashley."

"That's very kind, Mother." Ashley took a long breath. "Good news, by the way. I'm not the only one who's been running lines all week." She stayed still. "I believe Mr. Garrett's class is truly ready to visit Neverland tonight."

Ashley told Mom and Kari how her class had

practiced every day. Over and over on the days when props didn't work or Mr. Garrett had to keep Chris in line. "Also . . . a plus . . ." She flopped her hand around in front of her. "Landon's hook isn't flying across the room anymore."

"That's good." Mom held the curling iron in place. "Captain Hook isn't very menacing without his hook."

Kari giggled. "I can't wait to see it." She studied Ashley's hair. "You're becoming Wendy before our eyes!"

"Well . . ." Ashley gave her sister a look. "I already was Wendy. But now I'm more play-pared."

Mom set the curling iron down and picked up the hair spray. "Play-pared? What's that?" She shook the can.

"Prepared . . . but for a *play*." Ashley tapped her head. "Get it?"

"Hold your breath." Mom sprayed Ashley's hair. "You're the perfect Wendy."

Kari turned around and faced Ashley. "But it's just a little skit, right?"

"To some people." Ashley watched Mom fasten

the blue ribbon in her hair. Ashley looked at her reflection. "To me it's a lifetime, Kari. Neverland couldn't ever be just a little skit."

"I see." Kari smiled. "Are you nervous? About a lifetime in Neverland?"

"Nervous?" Ashley's look was complete. She stepped back and lifted her arms to her sides. "I can't wait."

"Good." Kari stood still as Mom began working on her makeup. Pink glitter for her eyelids and blush for her cheeks.

"I'm glad"—their mother kept her focus on Kari—"that this lifetime happens in just one night. I'd miss you, Ashley." Mom was good at playing along. "You know . . . if you moved to Neverland forever."

Ashley twirled round and round, her arms still out like she was flying. "You would come with us, Mom! You and Kari and Dad and the whole family!" The bathroom was spinning, so she stopped twirling. "Wouldn't that be a great adventure? And we would all stay young forever."

"Yes." Mom sighed a little. "That would be something."

Brooke popped her head into the bathroom. "Wow! You look so pretty, Ash."

"Thanks, Brooke." Ashley smoothed her dress. "It's a very twirly costume. Good for flying through Neverland."

"Okay." Brooke laughed. "Anyway, Dad wanted me to get you two. We're getting in the van." She yelled as she ran off, "Hurry, people! I could be doing homework right now if we didn't have this talent show."

When she was gone, Ashley looked at her mom and Kari. "Is it just me . . . or is Brooke acting very old these days?"

"She's fine." Mom put a few finishing touches on Kari's face. "She's just going through some tough classes. It's all part of growing up." Mom unplugged the curling iron and shut off the light. She led the way down the hall to the stairs.

Kari stayed close to Ashley's side as they trailed behind. "I'm worried about her." Kari sounded sad. "Brooke has to learn to do the next thing. The same way I did. Then she could enjoy the talent show instead of worrying about homework."

"Exactly!" Ashley could've stopped and hugged her sister. Finally someone agreed with her about staying young. She linked arms with Kari as they hurried to the van. "We all need to settle down and enjoy being kids."

In the van, most of the family was giddy with excitement about the talent show. Luke said he hoped someone did a basketball routine. "That's what I'm going to do when I'm old enough. I have it all figured out!"

Erin said she was going to sing a duet with one of her friends when she was old enough to be in the talent show.

"As thrilled as I am to officially be Wendy and . . . as ready as I am to take flight in Neverland"—Ashley pointed at Kari—"I cannot wait to see you and the Dancing Queens tonight! Your dance will be the hit of the show!"

Dad agreed, and Mom looked over her shoulder at them. "It'll be a night to remember."

Ashley peeked at Brooke, who sat in the back row studying her science flash cards. *Poor Brooke,*

Ashley thought. *And poor Kari, too.* Having so much homework and having to make so many decisions. Which reminded Ashley that she hadn't written out the Never Grow Up pledge. As they pulled up to the school, she made a promise to herself. She would write it tonight.

Before they got another day older!

Backstage was a zoo as Mr. Garrett wrangled everyone together for their portion of the night. Some of the students were at the snack table while a few made last-minute adjustments to their costumes.

Ashley went over her lines with Natalie, Elliot and Amy, who were dressed in their Tinker Bell, Peter Pan and Tiger Lily costumes.

One highlight was when Chris walked up in his baby blue footie pajamas. He had never looked younger. "Mr. Garrett!" Chris shouted and waved his hands. "I can't find my teddy bear! It's my only prop!"

Just then Landon walked up to Ashley. "Ahoy,

matey!" He used his best pirate growl and swished his hook in the air.

Ashley tugged at his hook. "Make sure that doesn't fly into the audience."

"My mom used duct tape." Landon made a face. "Hopefully it comes off when I *actually* need it to."

"If not, we can call you Landon Hook." Amy giggled. She took over the conversation. "Kinda sounds like your last name . . . Blake."

"Not really . . . not at all," Ashley muttered under her breath. *Rake* or *Break* sounded more like *Blake*. *Hook* did not.

Amy needed to work on her humor.

Even so, Landon's face lit up at the joke. Like it was the funniest thing he'd ever heard. "Good one, Amy." Landon used his normal voice now. "Hey, you play four square, right?"

"Yes, I do!" Amy beamed at Landon. "It's the best. I'm not as good as you, but I love to play."

"Well you should join us sometime at recess." Landon smiled at her. "If you want."

"That would be nice." Amy's cheeks turned red.

Ashley rolled her eyes at that girl. Then she

turned to Landon. "I play, too, Landon. And I'm *really* good."

Elliot was standing nearby in his Peter Pan costume. He looked confused. "You never play four square, Ashley."

"Yeah." Landon patted her curly head. "Very funny, Ash. Maybe stick to the three-legged race."

Ashley's mouth hung open. "I'm being confident here, okay?" She took a step closer to Landon. "I said I'm really good because that's what I believe. Whenever I do choose to play, I'll be very, very good." She crossed her arms. "That's called believing in yourself."

"Fine." Amy pulled Landon closer to her. "We'll let you play with us."

"Us?" Ashley noticed Landon was looking a little uncomfortable. "Amy . . . you can't just be part of an 'us.' Landon is my friend, not yours." She smiled at Amy. "Also, you may need Field Day practice before you can officially join in four square."

Natalie waved her wand this way and that. "Can we just move on? We have a show to do."

"Right. A show!" Ashley clapped. "Good, Natalie. Way to keep us in line." She held up her hands and raised her voice. "Let's go, people. We got a show to do. Places."

Mr. Garrett turned and stared at Ashley. "I'm the only one who can say 'Places.'" He cleared his throat. Then he looked around at the class. "Fine. Places, people! Let's circle up."

"I found it!" Chris ran up holding his teddy over his head. "I found the bear!"

"Wonderful." Mr. Garrett put his hands on his knees and caught his breath. He sounded a little worn out. "Boys and girls, here we are. After reading the book and . . . *much* rehearsal, I do believe we are ready to take the stage in two minutes!" He sighed. "Then come Monday we can put this whole thing behind us."

Put it behind them? Ashley studied their teacher. *Maybe he needs a part in the play,* she thought. *No one should be in a hurry to leave Neverland.*

Theirs was the first act so the whole class lined up backstage. Out in the auditorium, they heard Miss Patty welcome family and friends to the talent show.

Mr. Garrett dropped his voice to a whisper. "Okay, class. You can do this!" He looked at Ashley. "And stick to the script."

She saluted him. "I'll certainly try."

Miss Patty paused. "Now, ladies and gentlemen, please welcome to the stage Mr. Garrett's fifth-grade class presenting for you . . . *Peter Pan*."

The audience clapped and cheered, and moments later Ashley took her spot near the cardboard cut-out of a bed. The others took their places, too, as they waited for the curtain to rise. When it did, bright lights flooded the stage.

It was happening! Ashley could barely breathe. They were in Neverland! Amy took her spot at the center. An extra-bright light shone on her. "All children grow up . . . except one. This is the story of Peter Pan!" She threw a handful of pixie dust in the air. Then she began to tell the story of the Darling children and how one night Peter came to their window and told Wendy about his home in Neverland.

That was Elliot's cue.

He strutted onto the stage, fists on his hips.

"Neverland is the best place. A fantastic place where you never grow up!" Elliot was the most convincing Peter Pan ever.

Next it was Ashley's turn. She had never felt more like Wendy. "Oh, Peter!" She clasped her hands together. "Do take us with you! How do we get there?" The audience faded away. What was happening here felt as real as her next breath.

Elliot pointed out the window. "Second star to the right and straight on till morning."

"How amazing! I want to go!" Ashley ran to the window. Only her slippers slid on the wood floor and instead she lunged forward. Without warning, the window toppled to the ground, revealing a few pirates and Lost Boys, waiting their turn. Those students hurried out of sight.

The audience released a quiet laugh.

"Those pesky windows . . ." Ashley improvised. "Always being a pest. Falling over . . . and never opening when you need them to."

"I'll help!" Chris rushed in, his teddy bear flopping as he ran. Then he helped Ashley set the window back in its place.

"Thank you, Chris. That's very kind of you." Ashley patted Chris's head and gave him a gentle push back to his spot near the bed.

"I'm Michael." Chris scowled at her. "Not Chris."

More quiet laughter from the audience.

"True." Ashley waved at Chris. "Hello, Michael. You're very helpful with windows." She could practically feel Mr. Garrett staring at them from the wings. She did a curtsy toward Elliot. "Peter . . . how shall we get to Neverland?"

Elliot was frozen in place. He hadn't moved or spoken since the window incident. He glanced at the audience, and then back at Ashley, but still he said nothing.

Mr. Garrett's whisper was loud from just off-stage. "'We fly, of course!' That's your line!"

Elliot blinked a few times. "We . . . we fly, of course!"

The scene got back on track and the window stayed in place. They continued, accident-free. Even as they flapped their arms and flew to Neverland to meet the Lost Boys. And when Hook threatened to defeat Pan, good news! His hook stayed on.

In no time, it was the final scene. Ashley and the others were tied up to the pirate ship.

Amy continued her narration. "So, Wendy, her brothers and the Lost Boys watched Hook and waited for their fate."

Landon paced around the stage, sword in hand, hook high in the air. "Join the pirates or walk the plank!"

Elliot made the rooster crow sound and hopped onstage. "Peter Pan here, Hook. And I will defeat you!"

The audience hooted and hollered as Elliot and Landon fought with their prop swords. And, in one final move, Elliot pushed Landon off the ship, defeating Hook once and for all. The crowd applauded Pan's victory!

Next, Ashley was supposed to ask Peter to take them all home.

Only Ashley didn't want to go home.

She didn't want Wendy to return to London. Because she knew how the story ended. She had read the book. If she went home with her siblings,

Wendy would forget about Neverland and forget about her promise to stay young. Many years from now, Peter would return to the nursery window, crushed to see Wendy all grown up.

And Ashley didn't want any of that. She took a deep breath. What happened next was up to her!

"Peter Pan shall cut you free!" Elliot held up his sword to cut the ropes. "Then I will take you home to London!"

"No, you don't!" Ashley wiggled out of the ropes before he had the chance. "I got this, Pete." She threw the rope to the ground, freeing herself and the others.

Ashley gathered the children and moved them upstage. "Well . . . we got out of that!" She grinned at them. "What's next? Swim with the mermaids? Build another house?" She looked at the audience. "Fly around until we reach the end of the clouds?"

The crowd was starting to mumble. Ashley could see people looking at each other, possibly baffled. From backstage she heard Mr. Garrett's loud whisper. "Ashley! What are you doing! Stick with the script!"

"You know what's nice, Michael?" Ashley looked at Chris. "There's no script in Neverland."

"True, Wendy!" Chris grinned. "I like that about this place!"

Elliot walked up to Ashley. "Umm." His sword hung at his side. "Wendy. What are you doing?"

"We're not going home!" Ashley loved this idea. The Lost Boys looked happy about it, too. "So many adventures yet to take, Peter! And guess what? You can stay with us!"

The crowd chuckled.

It didn't take Elliot long to get on board. He shared a quick smile with Ashley and put his fists on his waist again. "Good! I didn't want to take you home in the first place." He looked at the other children. "And since I'm your leader, I will be in charge of a million adventures!"

Ashley ran to the ship's steering wheel. She surveyed the seas. "Peter, let's take the ship somewhere we've never been before!"

Chris pointed offstage. "That tall volcano, maybe!"

"Or that distant lake!" Elliot pointed the other direction.

"Wherever you want to take us, Peter." Ashley raised her fist in the air. "Let's never grow up." Ashley faced the crowd. She looked right at Brooke. "Let's stay this age forever!"

In the wings, Ashley caught a glimpse of Mr. Garrett. He had his hand over his eyes.

Amy, the narrator, looked unsure. But then she gave Ashley a happy look and took her spot again at the center of the stage.

She looked at the audience and laughed. "And so . . ." She glanced back at Ashley and the others. "Wendy and her brothers and all the Lost Boys stayed in Neverland with Peter Pan . . . where they . . . swam with mermaids . . . and flew on the clouds, and took their pirate ship from cove to cove looking for treasure." She was in her rhythm now. "And . . . they never, ever grew up."

Natalie fluttered from the wings to the spot where Ashley and the children stood. She sprinkled glitter over all of them and smiled at the crowd.

Ashley wasn't done yet. She put her arm around Natalie's shoulders and pointed to the audience. "We, Mr. Garrett's fifth-grade class, encourage you to do the same! Never grow up!"

The closing music played and Ashley and her classmates took their bows. The crowd clearly loved the new twist, because they were on their feet, clapping and cheering and taking pictures. Dad gave Ashley a thumbs-up and Ashley gave it back.

And then they hurried offstage. They had done it! The play was a success! In the back, even Mr. Garrett was clapping. He walked up to Ashley with a half smile. "You didn't stay with the script."

"It was better, though." Ashley did a nervous shrug. "Right, Mr. Garrett?"

He chuckled for a few seconds. "Actually . . . this time I think it was."

Landon tapped Ashley's shoulder. "That was awesome! You were like the Queen of Neverland. Great job, Ashley." He had to talk a little loud to be heard over the applause.

"Landon." Ashley put her hand on his shoulder. "That is my favorite compliment of all time. Thank you." She smiled at him, and he smiled back. "Good job, Hook. It's not easy for you to act mean." She stepped back. "Especially when I know the truth."

Ashley looked at Landon a few more seconds, and then Kari walked up. "Great work, Ash! I loved the new ending."

"Thanks!" Ashley stepped away from Landon and looked at her sister. "Are you next?"

"One more act, then us! Pray!" Kari motioned for Mandy and Liza to hurry up. "We're so nervous!"

Ashley closed her eyes as Kari and her friends ran off. "Help them, God," she whispered. "They're going to need it."

Just then Natalie ran up and grabbed her hand. "Come on! Mr. Garrett has pizza for us in the back room!"

"He does?" Ashley ran with Natalie to the room behind the stage. Back there all of Mr. Garrett's class was squealing and running around and celebrating.

As they ate pizza and talked about the show, Ashley thought of a drawing she would do later. In the picture, she would be the very person Landon Blake said she was. Her sword in the air and pixie dust falling all around her. She had to draw the picture, so she would remember forever the way she felt tonight.

Because Ashley Baxter truly was the Queen of Neverland.

19

Dancing Queens

KARI

Two minutes remained till they took the stage, and Kari and her friends were so nervous they could barely think. Kari had no idea how they were going to dance.

"I've never been so scared." Mandy's legs were shaking. "Why did I agree to this?"

Kari had to think of something fast. Suddenly she remembered the words her dad said earlier tonight. *Don't forget, Kari . . . you love dancing. So have fun!*

Yes, Kari told herself. Dad was right. They shouldn't be afraid. In a rush, Kari gathered Mandy and Liza close. "Look, girls . . . it's time for a pep talk."

Out on stage four sixth-graders were singing "Somewhere over the Rainbow." The song was almost over, so Kari didn't have long.

"Pep would be good." Liza's eyes were wide. "Did you see how many people are in those seats?"

"It doesn't matter." Kari looked intently at Liza and Mandy. "Listen! We've got this." She took hold of her friends' hands. "We've worked hard, we've practiced. We know the song!"

"Too well." Liza laughed. "I sing 'Under the Sea' all day long. My family's ready for something new."

Mandy's mom had brought sequined scarves to add to their costumes. Kari thought the addition was perfect. "No doubt we're the Dancing Queens tonight." She took a step back and twirled the ends of her scarf.

"True." Mandy adjusted the sequined scarf on her neck. "Dancing queens aren't afraid."

"There you go!" Kari gave Mandy a side hug.

"Not to mention . . ." Liza put her sunglasses on. "We look fabulous!"

"Oh yes we do!" Kari struck a pose and Mandy joined in. "Are we ready, Dancing Queens?"

"Yes!" Liza danced in place a bit. "Ready steady."

"Me, too." Mandy wasn't shaking now. "As ready as I'll ever be."

The rainbow singers were finished, and out on the stage, Miss Patty's voice rang through the building. "Give it up for Ms. Nan's Dancing Queens!"

"That's us! Go, go, go." Mandy pulled Kari and Liza onstage and they rushed to their starting positions, with their backs to the crowd.

Kari exhaled. This moment felt right. Being onstage. The thrill of the lights and the audience waiting for the show. Kari felt confident. She felt secure. Which was a feeling she hadn't felt in a while.

The music began, and the girls started their dance. Swaying one way and then the other, their hands in the air like long pieces of seaweed. At the same time they spun toward the front of the stage.

All three of them sang along to the music. The girls spread their arms in front of them. They wagged their fingers in unison.

Kari couldn't believe it. Their moves were in perfect time! Never had practice gone this well.

Also the bright lights made their pink and purple sequins extra shiny.

The song talked about the ocean floor and the girls stooped low and pretended to smooth out the sand. As they danced, the song came to life for Kari. Suddenly she knew without a single doubt what she wanted to be when she grew up.

She wanted to be a dancer! Kari Baxter *was* a dancer!

That was her career choice! What more *was* she looking for? And why hadn't she realized this sooner? It didn't matter. Kari's heart was full as they kept dancing.

Each girl had a solo dance spot in the song, and Mandy's came first. She danced across the stage, tossing her scarf and singing along. She pointed at some people in the audience for a few beats. From the second row, Mandy's parents looked so proud.

Liza was next. She skipped up toward Mandy, and did a turn as she hit center stage. She did a few kicks and then grabbed Mandy's hand, twirling her in and then out. Kari took over from there and for the next eight beats, she twirled and kicked.

They came together for the chorus. The song talked about having no troubles down in the bubbles. "Under the sea . . . under the sea . . ."

Finally they went into their own version of the electric slide. They sashayed to the right, and then to the left. In perfect timing, the girls took four steps back, one more forward, another back, then a hitch kick as they turned to the right, where they repeated the steps again.

The crowd cheered, and when the song came to an end, Kari and her friends struck their final pose—arms out, heads tilted back. The audience shouted and clapped for what felt like minutes.

Mandy, Liza and Kari took a bow. Kari was breathless. Not from dancing, but from this feeling. A feeling of accomplishment and purpose and knowing. Because up here tonight, she really did know exactly where she was supposed to be and what she wanted to do.

The girls waved to their families as they ran offstage. Miss Patty took her place again. "Give it up for the dynamic, fantastic Dancing Queens!" Miss Patty sounded like a professional. "Next up, we have some ventriloquism from Veronica Thomas!"

"I know what I want to be!" Kari took her friends' hands again and spun the group in a tight circle. "I want to be a dancer!"

"Of course!" Liza came to a stop and grinned at Kari. "We should've helped you think of that sooner!"

Kari couldn't decide which was better—the joy she felt from dancing in front of the crowd . . . or the relief in knowing what she wanted to be.

Mandy bounded around. "You'll be the best dancer the world ever knew!" She tossed the ends of her scarf. "That was so fun, Kari! Thanks for making us dance with you!"

Liza removed her sunglasses. "Hard to imagine how being a lawyer could be better than this."

"Kari!" Ashley ran up to her. "I saw the whole thing." She was eating a piece of pizza. "That was the most amazing, incredible, beautiful performance I have ever seen." She hugged Kari tight. "I'm so proud of you."

Kari closed her eyes. "Thanks, Ash." She was so grateful for this moment. And that she and her sister got to share the stage at their school's talent show. She raised her hands in the air. "And guess what?" Kari didn't wait for Ashley to guess. "I know what I want to be when I grow up!"

For a few seconds Ashley seemed to ponder the question. "A mermaid?"

"No, silly." Kari laughed. "A dancer! Ashley, I want to be a dancer!"

Ashley's whole face smiled. She put her hands on Kari's sequined shoulders and jumped a few times. "Of course! Because you already are a dancer!"

For the rest of the show, Kari and Ashley watched from the wings near Mandy and Liza. Veronica was hilarious, and Mac the Magician had greatly improved his act from the audition.

Darlene sang "Tomorrow" from *Annie*, and not every note was perfect. But she never stopped smiling, and that had to count for something.

"And now . . . for our final act . . ." Miss Patty sounded like she had the biggest secret. "Please give it up for the Terrific Three Teachers!"

What was this? Kari looked at Ashley. She'd never heard of this group. Darlene was supposed to be the last act of the night. Then from the opposite wings, three grown men made their way to the stage. They wore brightly colored disco outfits, long wigs and oversize sunglasses.

"Mr. Garrett!" Ashley nearly screamed as she hit Kari on the arm. "It's Mr. Garrett! And Mr. Stone!"

"And Mr. Chambers!" Liza and Mandy shouted at the same time.

Kari couldn't believe it. Sure enough, taking the stage were Ashley's teacher, the school's PE teacher and their principal. The intro music told Kari exactly what was about to happen. The song played on the radio all the time.

"ABC" by the Jackson 5!

Just like Kari and her friends, the men sang along with the song. But their moves were mostly disco slides across the stage and quick spins, which they did with a great deal of dramatic effect.

Who knew these guys were so talented! Or that they could pull off such a great surprise!

The three men ended the song and two other teachers popped confetti cannons over the audience. It was the most epic end to a talent show ever. Ashley and Kari, Mandy and Liza cheered from the side.

With the talent show officially finished, the lights came up and people started to mingle. Kari and Ashley ran with the other performers to the auditorium to find their families. The Baxters were easy to see.

They were in the front row.

"Congrats to our two stars!" Dad hugged Kari and Ashley and handed them each a single white rose.

Kari sniffed her flower and smiled. "Thank you!"

Mom pointed at Kari and then Ashley. "You girls were amazing! So proud."

"Ashley . . ." Luke stepped forward. "I like your new ending to *Peter Pan*. It should always be like that."

"I think Ashley took some artistic liberties." Brooke smirked.

Ashley looked proud. "Exactly. I thought it would be better if Wendy *didn't* grow up. What do you think about that, Brooke?"

Brooke laughed. "It was very entertaining."

"I can't wait for fourth grade so I can join the talent show!" Erin smiled at Kari and Ashley.

"We'll come watch you when it's your turn!" Kari hugged her younger sister.

"Kari!" Ms. Nan approached, clapping as she walked. She was with Brittany, a girl from Kari's class. The girl had done another fantastic dance routine in the show tonight. Ms. Nan put her arm around Kari's shoulders. "That was incredible. You looked like a star."

"Thank you, Ms. Nan!" Kari couldn't wait to tell everyone her career choice.

Ms. Nan looked at Brittany. "You know Britt?" She pointed at the girl. "She's in our class."

"Sure." Kari nodded. "Hi! You did great tonight!"

"Thanks!" Brittany handed Kari a flyer. "My mom has a dance studio. We do recitals and showcases. It's a lot of fun. I think you'd be really good!"

Kari looked at the flyer and her heart began to race. The pictures showed some kids dancing onstage and a beautiful room with bars and mirrors. It looked like a dream place. "You mean . . ." Kari looked at Brittany. "I could dance there? With you?"

"Yes." Britt grinned. "You're an incredible dancer!"

After all the doubts and not knowing from the past month, Kari felt something she hadn't expected. She felt her world falling into place.

"That looks great." Mom ran her hand over Kari's hair. "I think Kari would really enjoy taking dance lessons."

Kari smiled and looked at her classmate. "Thanks, Britt! See you Monday."

"See ya!" Britt ran off to find her family.

"Anyhoo." Ms. Nan adjusted her purse strap on her shoulder. "I don't want to keep you. Just thought I'd connect the dots."

Mom shook Ms. Nan's hand. "Thank you. We really appreciate you helping Kari."

"Kari's a great student." Ms. Nan turned to Kari. "Oh! Enjoy that meteor shower Sunday night. Can't wait to talk about it Monday!" Ms. Nan smiled and walked off.

"The meteor shower!" Kari whispered to herself.

With the buildup to the talent show, she had almost forgotten. This was the perfect weekend!

Dad gathered everyone and they walked back to the van. "Friday night . . . two celebrities fresh off their Bloomington debut." He smiled at Kari and Ashley. "I say we get ice cream."

Luke jumped up. "Yes! Chocolate chip!"

"You know, Kari girl." Mom took Kari's arm in hers. "You really were so good tonight. Like a professional."

"Which reminds me." Kari stopped short of the van and faced her family. "I know what I want to be when I grow up. God showed me up there on the stage!"

"Not a mermaid," Ashley whispered to the group.

Kari laughed. "No, not a mermaid." She took her time. "I want to be a dancer! More than being a doctor or a zookeeper or a politician or a lawyer. More than being a swimmer . . . I want to dance."

Dad was the first to pull her into his arms. "That's wonderful, Kari. I think dance lessons are definitely in order!"

Everyone congratulated her, and Mom squeezed her hand. "I knew the answer would come." Mom looked straight into her eyes. "I believe, Kari, you will be a very, very good professional dancer!"

"Thanks, Mom." Kari realized something. She would always need the support of her family. Now and when she was a professional dancer someday. Her family gave her one more reason to be thankful.

They had their fill of ice cream and back home they played with Bo before turning in for the night. Ashley was drawing in her sketchbook, so Kari decided to write her thoughts in her journal. The happiest thoughts she'd had in a long time.

Tonight was the talent show. Me and Liza and Mandy were the Dancing Queens and everyone loved us. And guess what? I decided during the show that I want to be a dancer! For a career! Then just to show me it was the right choice, a girl talked to me after and invited me to take dance lessons. Mom and Dad believe in my decision. And that's the best support a girl could have.

Good night.
KB

P.S. TWO DAYS UNTIL THE METEOR SHOWER!

20

Never Grow Up

ASHLEY

Today was a full day for Ashley. Not only was she going to Sunset Hills Adult Care Home with her mother and some other volunteers from church, but after that visit, they were going to Luke's first basketball game.

Which was why Ashley got up early to paint him a surprise sign. She sat at the kitchen table, working her paintbrush over a huge piece of cardboard.

Luke really was the best little brother Ashley and her sisters could ever have.

Right now he was outside dribbling his basketball. He told everyone he planned to do that for an hour before his game. Ashley was painting to the rhythm of the bouncing ball.

FWAP . . . FWAP . . . FWAP . . .

Ashley had already painted the letters for *GO LUKE!* Also she had added in a fine-looking basketball. Now she was working on painting NUMBER 1 on the poster.

"Morning . . ." Kari came into the kitchen and poured a bowl of cereal. "You're up early."

"Yeah!" Ashley held up the sign. "It's for Luke."

Kari took a bite of her breakfast. "I like it, Ash! Good job!"

Just then, Luke came in through the back door. His basketball was under his arm. "Whew!" He smiled at Ashley and Kari. "I'm thirsty!"

"Oh! Hello!" Ashley turned the sign over as fast as she could. "Don't you have . . . another hour of dribbling?"

"What's that?" Luke pointed at Ashley's sign.

"Nothing." She spread herself across the sign. "Just me and the table here. Nothing to see." She forced a smile.

"Are you making a sign for my game?" Luke grinned as he took a drink of water.

Ashley shrugged and then zipped her lips shut and threw away the key.

"That's really nice, Ashley. Thanks." Luke took another drink and he laughed. "Because I can see the cardboard."

Kari took the seat next to Ashley. "Are you excited for the game?"

"You know it!" Luke dribbled the ball on the kitchen floor a few times. "When I grow up I'm gonna be in the NBA! I have to be ready!"

Ashley felt her mouth fall open. There it was again! Another sibling looking to grow up too fast. What was with everyone? She wanted to tell Luke to put the basketball away and skip his game. Go out back and look for frogs or lizards.

But she didn't want to ruin his happy day. So she kept her thought to herself. Besides, she had zipped her lips and thrown away the key.

Luke moved to the sink for more water. Just then, Mom walked into the kitchen buttoning up her jacket.

"Ashley, dear. We need to go." She grabbed her

purse. "It's chilly this morning . . . you should get your coat."

"Already?" Ashley glanced at Luke and then back at Mom. "I just need a few more minutes." She stood on her chair and pointed down at the cardboard sign. "Just a few . . . more . . . minutes."

Mom's eyes said she was clearly confused. "Ashley . . . you know we don't stand on chairs."

"Mother." Ashley dropped to the floor and looked hard at her mom. Luke was facing the table now. He could see everything. This time Ashley held up one hand for cover, and then secret-like she again pointed to the sign. "I am not . . . quite ready. Get it?"

"No." Mom shook her head. "Honey . . . we don't have time."

Ashley used her head to gesture for her mom to come over. Mom did, but she did not look amused.

"What's going on?" Mom stared at her. "What are you pointing at?"

Ashley threw her hands in the air. "Fine." She flipped the cardboard over. "Don't look, Luke."

He cheered and put both hands straight up. "Yes! I knew it was for me."

"It was a surprise." Ashley frowned. "Which is now ruined."

"Oh . . . I'm sorry." Her mom kissed her cheek. "You can finish it later. We really have to go."

Ashley found her coat in the front closet and ran after Mom to the van. On the way there, Ashley turned to her mother. "I have a few questions for you."

"Okay." Mom looked more relaxed now that they were driving. "Ask away."

"First." Ashley turned so she was facing her mother. "Exactly how old are these people?"

"It depends." Mom kept her eyes on the road. "Two are in their seventies. Another couple are in their eighties. I believe there is one woman in her nineties and I've heard that one man at Sunset Hills is a hundred and three."

"Wow! That's old. He must have a lot of wisdom." Ashley put her hand to her head. "Next . . . are we gonna get to play dominoes with these old people?"

Mom shot her a glance. "The elderly, Ashley. Yes. We will play dominoes with them."

"The elderly." Ashley tapped her chin. "I'll try to remember that." She sighed. "Why do we need to visit them? Don't they have families?"

"Some do." Mom turned in to the driveway of what looked like an old house. "Some of them don't have family in the area."

Ashley gasped. "They're lonely! That's why we're here." She shook her head. "That's so sad." *If only these people had signed a pledge when they were in fifth grade,* she thought.

"It can be . . . ," Mom continued. "But there are great benefits to a place like this. The people here are in a community going through the same things. And they have people taking care of daily issues for them."

"What kinds of issues?" Ashley tugged at her seatbelt.

Mom thought about this for a moment. "Well, like bills or dishes or laundry. Sometimes you get to a point where you've done enough of that!"

"No chores? No bills? A bunch of friends and games?" Ashley shook her head in amazement.

"Sounds like these people are more like kids than grown-ups!"

Mom laughed. "I guess you're right."

When they walked inside, the woman who worked at Sunset Hills showed them around. Six elderly people lived here, she told them. The tour ended in the dining room, where Mom sat with three women at the table.

Ashley moved to the living room and played Connect Four with a man named Carlos. Next she found a cozy chair by the fireplace. A woman in a wheelchair sat there, rubbing her hands together. "It's always cold," she said. "But today things feel a little warmer."

The woman looked friendly She had silver hair and dark brown eyes. "Hi." Ashley kicked her legs. Her feet didn't quite touch the ground. "I'm Ashley Baxter."

The woman turned to Ashley. "I'm Dot." She smiled.

"That's a nice name." Ashley nodded. "Short. Simple." She shrugged one shoulder. "Wanna be friends? I'm pretty good at it."

"At being friends?" Dot sounded surprised. She leaned back a bit in her wheelchair.

Ashley nodded. "Yep. I made a lot of new friends this year. 'Cause we moved. So apparently I'm good at it."

"How do you make a new friend?" Dot crossed her wrists on her lap. Her hands were wrinkled with brown spots. On one wrist was a pretty pearl bracelet. It matched the pearl earrings she wore.

Ashley studied Miss Dot. She was . . . kind of glamorous. Ashley took a deep breath. "Well . . . you have to ask questions. Like . . . 'Miss Dot? Do you like gymnastics?' for example." Ashley blinked a few times, waiting for a reaction. "So do you?"

"Are you asking or is it an example?" Dot looked at Ashley over the eyeglasses resting on her nose.

"Both." Ashley paused. "Do you?"

Dot laughed. "I did cheerleading in school. We had to do some tumbling work. But I never did much gymnastics. I was a singer." Her eyes twinkled. She looked like she had the most exciting secrets.

Ashley couldn't wait to hear them! "A singer!" She jumped out of her chair, scooted it closer to

Dot and shifted it so it faced her. Then she plopped back down. "Tell me *everything*."

Dot took a deep breath. "Well . . . it was a long time ago." She paused. Like she was seeing those days all over again. Finally Dot began her story. "I used to live in New York City. And I would sing in the jazz clubs. Billie Holiday songs. Oh . . . I wanted to be her when I grew up." Dot shook her head.

"I've heard of Billie Holiday!"

"You have?" Dot sounded very surprised.

"Mhmmm. Our music teacher, Miss Patty, talked about her in choir." Ashley pulled a stray hair behind her ear.

Miss Dot kept remembering. "Billie was a legend. They called her Lady Day." Then Dot looked into the fire and smiled for a while. Eventually she looked back at Ashley. "Anyway. I would sometimes sing Billie Holiday songs. At parties and restaurants and jazz clubs . . ." Her voice trailed off.

Miss Dot had mentioned that Billie Holiday detail two times. Ashley wasn't sure if Miss Dot remembered that. *Best not to say anything*, she thought.

Ashley wanted to know more. "Did you ever travel? As a singer?"

"Yes. I was a professional singer for over a decade. From the East Coast to the West Coast and all the way to Ireland and India. I sang jazz for the troops." Dot held a finger in the air. "I even got to do a performance for the Queen of England."

"Wow! The queen?" Ashley stood. "Did you have to curtsy, like this?" She threw her hands in the air and bent at the waist. Her nose nearly hit the floor.

"That's not a curtsy, little miss!" Dot laughed out loud.

"Oh." How many times had Ashley done a curtsy wrong?

"I'll teach you." Miss Dot pointed. "Tuck your left leg behind you, grab your skirt and do a little bow of the head."

Ashley looked at her jeans. "I don't have a skirt."

"That's okay." Dot smiled. "You can pretend."

Ashley did her best curtsy. "Thank you, madam. I won't forget that."

"Curtsies have gone out of style, I'm afraid."

Miss Dot rubbed her hands together again.

Ashley wanted more of Dot's story. "So . . . what else did you do? After all your touring?"

Dot thought about this. "I studied music. After that, I continued singing. But in the church." She shrugged. "To be honest . . . I enjoyed settling down and singing in the choir after all those years on the road."

"What was your favorite song?" Ashley sat on the floor at Miss Dot's feet. She studied everything about that beautiful and kind old woman.

Miss Dot didn't hesitate. "'Blue Moon.' It was a Billie Holiday song."

"What?" Ashley squealed. "I know that song! We learned it in choir!"

And then Dot started to sing the song. Her sweet voice still sounded clear as a bell. Ashley could picture herself in New York City listening to Dot sing on a stage.

Ashley joined in with Dot. They were a couple of stars. They reached the end of the song and the two of them applauded themselves.

It was a special moment.

"Very good voice, dear." Dot patted Ashley's shoulder. "Thanks for singing with me. I liked that very much."

"Thanks for letting me! I'm honored to share this moment with a famous star!" Ashley stood. "Why don't you sing more! You're so good." She took gentle hold of Dot's hand.

"Oh, Ashley. No one cares to hear a ninety-year-old woman croak old jazz standards." Dot shook her head. "I don't know how getting this age happened. One day I was selling out shows and the next day . . . I was married. We raised two children." Her smile faded. "Then they were grown up and moved away. My husband died ten years ago." Her eyes looked sad. "You wake up one morning and you're an old woman." She gave Ashley's hand a slight squeeze. "Life moves very fast."

"Tell me about it." Ashley thought about Dot's story. She knew all too well what Dot was talking about. "My siblings are in a rush to grow up. I'm just trying to get them to relax a little!"

"That's the key. Slow down. Enjoy life." Dot winked at Ashley. "And sing whenever you can."

"I'll keep that in mind." Ashley saw Mom getting her coat on. Ashley smiled at Dot. "I have to leave now. We are going to my brother's basketball game. But it was nice meeting you." She held her hand out.

Dot shook it. "Good meeting you, too."

"See you next time?" Ashley pointed at her new friend.

"I look forward to it." Dot pointed back.

As Ashley walked out of Sunset Hills with Mom, she looked around, and a thought came to her. The people at Sunset Hills used to be kids. They used to have dreams and go on adventures. And one day, like Dot, they grew up. Would she and her siblings actually end up here? With only the memories of what used to be?

And suddenly Ashley could feel the clock ticking.

They needed a meeting at the rock as soon as possible.

Luke scored thirteen points in his game—more than anyone else.

Ashley figured her sign had something to do with his great game. He also got ten *ribbons* in the first half. Though Ashley didn't ask Dad about that till the game was over. "Where are his ribbons?" She squinted at the boys and their coach down on the floor. "Mom said he had ten ribbons in the first half."

"Rebounds, honey." Dad gave her a silly look. "Can you imagine the basketball players wearing ribbons?" He pointed to the hoop. "Someone shoots and misses, and someone else grabs the ball. That's called a rebound."

Ashley thought she'd rather have a ribbon. But, then, basketball was Luke's game. If he wanted these rebounds, so be it. Whatever made him happy.

The drive home took forever. Ashley couldn't wait to get down to business. She ran to her room and grabbed a page from her sketchbook. Then she wrote out the pledge:

To the rest of the world:
We, the Baxter Children, believe in Neverland.
And so we promise here and now to never
grow up! To never put jobs before each other.

And to never forget to have fun.
Signed:
Ashley Baxter

Beneath that she drew four lines where her siblings could sign. And below that, she drew a sketch. A pirate ship with all five Baxter kids sailing off to Neverland.

Ashley grabbed the contract. They had no time to lose. She ran through the house gathering Brooke and Kari, Erin and Luke. "Hurry! To the rock," she yelled.

The rock was the special place they had discovered the week they moved into their new home. It sat near the stream in a clearing, behind a row of trees at the back of their property. They had painted the rock with their names and handprints and decided it was the perfect place to meet when they needed to have a serious talk.

Like the one Ashley wanted to have today.

She slipped through the trees and took the lead to the rock. As she scrambled up, she ran her fingers over the painted handprints and their names. Then she waited for the others.

Kari poked her head through the trees next. She climbed up on the rock and squinted at Ashley. "Why were you running so fast?"

"Yeah." Luke scrambled up, too. "Good thing I'm an athlete."

"I need water . . ." Erin followed him.

Brooke was last. "I need oxygen." She joined everyone on the rock.

Ashley stood up. It was time. "Attention, Baxter Children." She was loud enough that everyone listened. "It has been a busy few weeks. The talent show, the 5K, Career Day." She looked at each of them. "I feel like life is moving too fast. Anyone else?"

Kari raised her hand. "I like being a sixth grader."

"Maybe . . ." Luke tapped his chin and squinted his eyes. "But, then again . . . maybe not? I can't be in the NBA unless life moves faster."

"I don't mind fast. Since Christmas is coming." Erin clasped her hands.

"Sure, we've been busy." Brooke shrugged. "But it's just life, Ash."

"No." Ashley stomped her foot. "It's not just life, Brooke. We know you're going to grow up and go to medical school. And Kari may be a famous dancer, and Erin will teach children—even though she's just a child herself. And Luke will be in the NBA, and I will, I will . . . do something amazing, I'm sure."

Ashley took a quick breath. "But right now . . ." She paused and crouched down. "Right now, life is moving too fast." She studied their faces. "And I don't want to wake up one day with gray hair and only memories of a life I barely remember."

Kari raised her hand. "Where is this coming from, Ash?"

Ashley held out the piece of paper. "This . . . is a pledge. A contract."

"Oooh!" Luke ran up to it. "What for?"

Ashley held the page out and read it: "To the rest of the world: We, the Baxter Children, believe in Neverland. And so we promise here and now to never grow up! To never put jobs before each other. And to never forget to have fun. Signed . . ." She paused. "This . . . is a Never Grow Up Contract." She felt good about this. "Now you four have to sign it."

"A Never Grow Up Contract?" Brooke raised her eyebrows as she walked closer. "How does *that* work?"

"Like I said . . . we sign our names." Ashley pointed at the paper. "I already did mine."

No one said anything.

Ashley tried again. "Get it? We decide here and now that we will stay . . . just the way we are. That we will never grow up." Her voice got louder and she raised one fist. "That we will be like this rock. Solid. Together. The five of us forever." She lowered her hand. "What do you say?"

"Hmm." Luke grabbed the pen. "Do you think I can sign this and still make it to the NBA?"

Ashley thought about that. "I'm not sure about the specifics."

Luke shrugged and signed his name. Erin signed next. She smiled. "Young forever! That's me." She handed the pen to Kari. "Your turn."

"Well . . ." Kari bit the tip of the pen. "Is it possible? We just . . . decide?"

"I don't know for sure." Ashley pointed to the pledge. "But I feel really good about it." She looked at Kari. "We have to try."

Kari nodded. "You're right." She signed her name. "I can do that. I promise to never grow up."

"Good." Ashley took the pen and held it out to Brooke. "What about you, Miss Med School?" Ashley figured Brooke would be the hardest to convince. She had basically planned out her entire life.

Brooke looked around the circle. "I love you all and I'd do anything for you." She looked at Ashley.

"Sure, I have goals and dreams. But you matter more." She took the pen. "I'm in." She signed the pledge.

"Wow . . ." Ashley couldn't believe it. Everyone had signed the contract. "We did it."

Brooke handed the contract back to Ashley and she studied it. Then she looked at her sketch of Captain Hook's ship, headed for Neverland. Ashley hopped off the rock, walked over to one of the trees. She pulled a stapler from her jeans pocket and stapled the contract to the trunk.

The perfect end to a perfect ceremony.

"Kids! Dinner is ready!" Mom's voice carried through the trees.

Luke jumped down from the rock and took off. "Spaghetti!" Kari and Erin followed.

Only Brooke and Ashley stayed behind. Brooke took Ashley's hand. "The pledge is perfect, Ashley. I needed to be reminded . . . to slow down."

"We all do." Ashley put her head on Brooke's shoulder. "Now come on, Brooke . . . let's go get some pie."

They walked back to the house, giggling. And

Ashley felt like she could live in this weekend forever. And thanks to the contract . . . she could. They all could. They would do what everyone thought was impossible. Everyone except one boy named Peter.

They would never grow up.

21

Meteors and Memories

KARI

After weeks of counting down, the big moment had finally arrived. And, in just a few hours, at about eight o'clock tonight, Kari would finally see her very first meteor shower.

There was something else that made today special. Through many guesses and moments of anxiety, and after looking at many options, she finally knew what she wanted to be when she grew up. She had already written her outline.

Life of a Professional Dancer, she titled it.

But she added something else. A surprise that just sort of popped into her head on the way home from church.

Kari flopped on her bed, pulled out her notebook and went to work. When I grow up, I want to be a professional dancer and . . .

Someone knocked at the door.

"Yes?" Kari looked up from her journal. "Come in."

Dad opened the door and stared at Kari. "Hey . . . I wanted to talk to you."

Right away Kari could tell something was off. "Okay." She sat up straighter and set down her notebook.

Dad sat on the edge of her bed. Then he sighed a very heavy sigh.

"Is everything okay?" Kari felt suddenly concerned.

"It's about Alex Hutchins." He looked out the window, and back to Kari. His eyes were soft and watery. "Alex . . . his health declined earlier this week. He needs to stay in the hospital longer than they thought."

"No." Kari didn't want to believe it. "So he can't come watch the meteor shower with us?"

Dad shook his head. "No, sweetheart."

"Is he going to get better?" Kari felt tears in her eyes. She slid next to her dad and held him real tight. "I thought we raised enough money for him. . . . I thought he was getting better."

Dad ran his fingers over Kari's hair. "We did. And that money helped his family. But Alex is just still really ill."

"But . . . we prayed." Kari looked at her dad.

Dad looked at her. "And we will keep praying. We have to trust God, even when we don't get the answer we want." Dad took a deep breath. "That's called faith."

Kari closed her eyes. She didn't understand. But she knew Dad was right. She could trust God . . . even when it didn't make sense. If Dad could still have faith, then so could Kari.

Dad stood. "Luke and the girls are playing basketball. He said he'd love for us to join him for a game of HORSE."

Kari hesitated. And it occurred to her that life was really special. How often did she wake up and take the morning for granted? She never wanted to forget about the gift of today. Because some people were sick in hospitals.

"I'm gonna go outside." Dad kissed the top of

Kari's head. "See you out there?" He headed out of the room.

A minute later, Mom popped her head in. "Dad told you about Alex?"

"He did." Kari thought for a moment. "Let's go see him again next week."

"Okay." Her mom pointed to the notebook on the bed beside Kari. "Working on your essay?"

"Trying." Kari picked up her pencil. "I know something else I want to do."

"What's that?" Mom's voice sounded lighter. A nice change from the sadness about Alex.

Kari held up the open notebook. "When I grow up . . . I want to be a professional dancer and . . . I want to be me."

Mom raised her eyebrows. "You want to be . . . yourself?"

"Yes." Kari loved this. "See . . . people have said I am fun, creative and a good friend. Those are my three supporting points. And that's who I want to be. I could be a dancer. But maybe not." She felt great about this. "Whatever my job, I want to be Kari Baxter. The girl who is fun, creative and a great friend."

"I love it." Mom paused. "I think yours will be Ms. Nan's favorite essay."

Kari nodded. "Me, too."

Mom stood. "If grown-up you is like young you, then the world is in for a treat."

"Thanks." Kari almost told Mom about the contract. But that could wait. Plus it was just for the five Baxter children.

"Okay." Mom smiled. "We'll be outside when you're ready." She left and shut the door behind her.

Kari started to write again, but the project made her feel like she was going against the promise to never grow up. She closed her notebook. There was still time. For now, her homework could wait.

Kari hopped off her bed, and joined her family outside at their basketball hoop. The game hadn't started yet. For the next hour they all took turns doing trick shots and goofy free throws. They ate chicken and squash, and before Kari knew it, they were all seated on a blanket in the backyard, eating Mom's fresh-baked pumpkin cookies and drinking hot chocolate.

This was the moment Kari had been waiting for! The meteor shower was about to begin.

"I can't believe it's finally here . . ." Kari stared at the sky. It was still too early. But she didn't want to miss any of it. She took another cookie. "I'm so excited."

"Why are you so excited?" Luke sat beside her.

"Because, I've never seen a meteor shower." Kari took a sip of her hot chocolate. "I think it sounds spectacular."

"I've always wanted to see one, too." Mom sat next to Dad, both of them in lawn chairs.

Brooke took a cookie from the tray. "Carly said she and her family are watching it, too."

"Yeah." Luke waved his hands in the air. "I bet the whole world is watching."

Erin was lying on her stomach, reading. "The whole world can't watch. It's about to be daytime somewhere else."

"Okay." Luke laughed. "The whole city then."

Ashley had been quiet for the past few minutes. She pointed to the darkening sky. "I just wonder if we'll see the second star to the right." She rested her head on Kari's shoulder, and hugged her knees. "I'm glad we're doing this. Just in case."

Kari leaned her head against her sister's. "Me, too."

The sun had now completely set and the first few twinkles of stars were coming out.

Dad went back to the house and returned with more blankets. "Here . . . it's getting cold."

Kari and Ashley shared one.

"Seven fifty-five!" Mom almost sang out the announcement. "Any minute now."

Kari didn't look down. She didn't want to miss any of this.

Suddenly streaks of light began zipping across the dark sky. One. Then two. Then another few. With each one, Kari's mouth dropped a little more. A bright one fell vertically toward the ground, and it gave her goose bumps. Twinkling lights indicated that some were further away. A few of the meteors had long tails, while others didn't have tails at all.

The meteor shower was the most beautiful light show Kari had ever seen.

No one said anything.

The tails coming off the meteors were a wide range of unexplainable colors. Kari felt overwhelmed with awe and gratitude. All this waiting . . . and tonight one of her dreams was coming true.

Ashley studied the sky. "I sort of feel like a meteor."

"You?" Kari kept her eyes on the sky. "Why?"

"It's all of us." Ashley sighed. "Shooting across the sky . . . going through life so fast . . ."

"I like that, Ash." Brooke's words were barely loud enough to be heard. "Enjoy the beautiful now . . . while we can."

Kari's eyes were still on the sky. Maybe Alex had a view of the amazing show from his hospital room.

A few more meteors whizzed overhead, making their way through outer space. The same way that Kari was finding her way through life. She hadn't thought about it until Ashley brought it up.

Kari hoped wherever she went, she left a beautiful streak of light, too.

The meteors were fading away, meaning the show was almost over. For a few more moments, everyone stayed still and quiet.

Luke was resting his head on his basketball. Erin's book was closed. Brooke blinked a few times, studying the stars and petting Bo, who rested near her. Ashley played with some grass and Kari looked back at her parents. Even though they were sitting in separate lawn chairs, they were cuddled together under one blanket. It was a perfect ending to a very special day.

Kari stared at the sky. She never wanted to forget this moment. The final meteors reminded her of her family. Burning bright till the very end. And because of faith and love, doing what the Baxter family did best. The same thing the meteors had done.

Being very bright lights in the darkness.

22

Us Five

ASHLEY

Ashley was still watching the sky. She picked at the grass that overlapped onto the blanket she shared with Kari. The meteor shower had been spectacular. Which was a spelling word for next week in Mr. Garrett's class.

Spectacular.

Yes, that described everything about this weekend. She was deep in thought. So much had happened over the past few weeks. She was glad for a night to just rest and reflex. Or maybe it was *reflect*.

Either way, that's where she was. In her head, thinking about Neverland and Landon's compliment. Sunset Hills Adult Care Home and Luke's game . . . and all the adventures ahead.

She looked at her sisters and brother, glad they had all made a decision to stay young. They sat there, under the starry sky, in total silence.

The quiet of the night was rare. Especially for her family.

But tonight, there was no game, no talent show, no practice or homework assignment. No church event or party to attend. Tonight was just real life stopping for a meteor shower. Just the gift of sharing something special with the people she loved.

"You know," Ashley whispered. "This family is pretty spectacular."

It was true. The way Mom and Dad kept everything running and were there to celebrate every moment—even this one. The way Brooke had joined them at the rock yesterday even when she had homework. How Kari brought music and laughter to the family, and Erin added a layer of quiet and depth. And how Luke made every day a little more fun.

Even Bo did a great job being everyone's friend. Despite his thievery.

Yes, her family was definitely spectacular.

Just in case there was enough light from the moon, Ashley had brought her sketchpad.

Pictures, stories, and movies of meteor showers never looked like the sky tonight. Because God would always be the best artist.

Ashley looked up at the stars again. They twinkled and winked at her from their places in the sky. She saw one that burned brighter than the others. Maybe that was the star Peter Pan had talked about.

A nearby owl did a loud HOOT! And it was followed up with a howl. Probably those crazy old wolves. A few weeks ago, the sound would have scared Ashley. But now . . . now the sounds were part of home. They comforted her and sang her to sleep each night.

She could feel her neck cramping. Her head was still resting on Kari's. But Ashley didn't want to move. She didn't want the moment to end. This very special meteor moment.

"Well . . ." Dad broke the silence. "I am going to clean up the kitchen." He stood, stretched and folded his chair. "That was an extraordinary show. Thanks, Kari. For keeping the countdown going."

He made his rounds, squeezing shoulders and kissing foreheads. "Love you, kiddos. More than anything."

Mom stood as well and Dad grabbed her chair, too. "I'll come help." Mom touched Ashley's head. "Love you, kids."

Brooke sighed and moved to her feet. "I should probably go inside, too. I still have homework."

Ashley felt a sudden panic. "No, Brooke. Please stay!"

Mom put her hand on Brooke's shoulder. "Stay, honey. For a few more minutes. Homework can wait."

Brooke settled back down onto the blanket. "You're right. I'll stay." She motioned for Ashley and the others to spread out. "Lay on your backs. Let's look at the stars!"

Forever Ashley would remember Brooke staying with them this way. She and Kari and Erin and Luke all did as she said.

"It's kinda chilly!" Erin's teeth chattered.

Ashley handed her one of the blankets. "Here. This will help."

"The moon looks like a basketball." Luke pointed up. "I bet I could slam dunk on the moon. No gravity."

"True. It would be a boring game, though." Brooke slowed down her words. "Everyone . . . would . . . play . . . in . . . slow . . . motion."

Erin giggled. "That *would* be boring. You think there are animals up there?"

"What would they eat?" Kari looked at Erin.

"Cheese!" Luke's voice echoed through the backyard, making him and all the sisters laugh out loud. "The moon's made of it. At least, that's what one of the kids in my class said."

Erin sat up a little and looked at Luke. "I bet moon cheese is good."

"I don't think it's cheese." Brooke was still laughing.

Ashley turned to Brooke. "What exactly is it?"

"Well . . . technically it's a rock. And it's white 'cause the sun shines on it. So, it looks like it's glowing in the dark, but actually it's just being lit up by the sun." Brooke paused. "I read about it in my science book." She turned back to Kari. "What do you think it is?"

Kari looked up. "I think it's God's night-light." She turned to Ashley. "What about you, Ash? What do you think it is?"

Hmm, Ashley thought. The moon seemed like a lot more than a big rock. She smiled at her sister and then she looked up at the moon for a long time. She thought about how big it was. How bright it was. And then she thought about Dot. And the song. The moon really was so special. They wrote movies and songs about it. People put the moon in books and in jokes. She thought how the moon could be seen at some point by people all over the world.

In fact, maybe tonight, her Michigan friend, Lydia, was staring at the moon, too. For that matter maybe Landon and Natalie, Elliot and Mr. Garrett and even Chris were looking at the moon right now. The same one Ashley and her siblings were looking at.

Which made Ashley feel like they were with her somehow.

In her heart.

She pictured Dot staring at the moon tonight singing her "Blue Moon" song. Yes. The moon really was special.

"Ashley? Did you hear the question?" Kari looked over at her. "What do you think it is?"

"The moon?" Ashley took a breath. "It's Neverland. I think it really might be."

They were all quiet, thinking about that. Erin broke the silence. "Look! That star cluster looks like Mom's cat clock!" Erin pointed up.

Ashley laughed. Erin was right! The stars looked just like the clock they'd bought and then broke . . . for Mom's birthday.

"That gift was a cat-astrophe." Luke's joke made all of them laugh out loud.

Brooke pointed another direction. "The Big Dipper!"

Ashley grabbed her sketchbook.

"What are you doing?" Kari rolled onto her side and watched.

"I have to get this down." Ashley took a pencil and began to sketch. "Before I forget."

"What is it?" Kari put her hands under her head.

Ashley didn't answer. She was lost in thought. Thanks to the moonlight, she could see the paper clear as day . . . so she got to work. She wanted to draw tonight. Her siblings, from God's viewpoint. She sketched them all on their blanket, heads close, watching the meteor shower.

Still young. Still together.

If she didn't finish the sketch, she might forget.

And when kids forget what it's like to be young, they wake up one day as adults.

"I wanna see it!" Kari poked Ashley's shoulder. "Show me."

Ashley stared at the drawing. She loved it.

"Here." She turned it around and showed it to Kari. Brooke and Luke sat up to see it, and Erin climbed over Kari to get a better view.

"Wow. Ash . . ." Kari's eyes grew wide.

"It's us." Luke said in a tone so soft and sweet, it almost sounded poetic.

Brooke reached over and squeezed Ashley's hand. "It's perfect."

"Look!" Kari gasped and pointed up. "A shooting star!" They all laid on their backs again, keeping their eyes open for more.

They spent a few more minutes laughing and stargazing and dreaming. Doing what they liked to do best as Baxter children. And in that moment, Ashley knew her contract had worked.

The worry of Monday, the stress of school, and the weight of adult life were nowhere in sight. One day they would have to answer life's big questions.

They would have to carry heavy things. And pay bills. And fight monsters in the closet. But not tonight.

Tonight, they were exactly where they were supposed to be.

And, even if somewhere deep down Ashley knew that being a kid wouldn't last forever, she was grateful they had right now, here, when the meteors were still streaking across the sky. And she was thankful they had each other. Because that was enough.

That would always be enough.

About the Authors

Karen Kingsbury, #1 *New York Times* bestselling novelist, is America's favorite inspirational storyteller, with more than twenty-five million copies of her award-winning books in print. Her last dozen titles have topped bestseller lists, and many of her novels are under development as major motion pictures. Her Baxter Family books are being developed into a TV series. Karen is also an adjunct professor of writing at Liberty University. She and her husband, Donald, live in Tennessee near four of their adult children.

Tyler Russell has been telling stories his whole life. In elementary school, he won a national award for a children's book he wrote, and he has been writing ever since. In 2015, he graduated college with a BFA from Lipscomb University. Soon after, he sold his first screenplay, *Karen Kingsbury's Maggie's Christmas Miracle*, which premiered in December of 2017 on the Hallmark channel. Along with being an author of screenplays and novels, Tyler is a songwriter, singer, actor, and creative who lives in Nashville, Tennessee, where he enjoys serving his church, adventuring around the city, and spending time with his family.